I0744117

SUGARCOATED

HANSEL AND GRETEL'S
WITCH...
WASN'T
K.M. ROBINSON

SUGARCOATED

Copyright © 2018 by K.M. Robinson.

Published by Crescent Sea Publishing.
www.crescentseapublishing.com

Cover designed by Reading Transforms.
Image copyright © K.M. Robinson Photography.

This is a work of fiction. Names, characters, brands, trademarks, places, and incidents either are the product of the author's imagination or are used fictitiously. Any resemblance to actual events, locales, organizations, or persons, living or dead, is entirely coincidental and beyond the intent of either the author or the publisher.

*To those who took on the responsibility when they didn't
have to.*

CHAPTER 1

Sweets give us the illusion of happiness, beckoning us to sample brightly-colored sugar treats and revel in their sweetness…until they destroy us from the inside out and make our worlds crumble.

"Your brother will be here soon," I remind the small girl. "You need to get into position before he arrives."

"Annika, really? Can't we just wait until we see him coming?" She heaves a sigh as she traipses back over to the container. The blonde girl lifts her foot, nearly tangling herself in her skirt.

"You need to get used to it if you're going to help the

cause, Gretel. You'll be in there for a long time." I almost hope my words might convince her to walk away from this mission—killing the king is no place for a little girl. The other half of me knows that she is our only chance at ending this.

"You sound like my brother," she grumbles.

"Yes, and *you* look like him," I snip at her, grinning. "Now, in."

Gretel drops down into the barrel that used to contain flour, her blonde braids dipping below the rim. I set the lid on, leaving just enough space so that air can flow in and out. If there's time, I'll inch the lid over before Hansel comes to collect her.

I walk gently over to the window, lecturing Gretel on the importance of controlling her breathing in small spaces while I keep an eye out for her brother. Just like every day for the past three months, he should be arriving any moment from the woods after work.

Right on cue, he saunters down the path, pack over his shoulder. I duck behind the curtain before he has a chance to notice me. Scurrying over to where Gretel is hiding in the barrel by the fireplace, I bump the lid.

"Showtime," I whisper to myself. Lifting my hand, I brush back a piece of hair. In my peripheral vision, I notice a bit of flour on my hand from the barrel—I imagine Gretel will come out white as a ghost. We'll have to clean her off before she leaves so we aren't discovered.

"Annika," Hansel regards me as the door swings open. His tall frame fills the doorway, and I feel myself blush as he smiles. "Is Gretel ready?"

"You can take her home if you can find her," I reply, turning away from him. I busy myself kneading bread.

Hansel sighs heavily, dropping the bag on the ground by the table leg. I glance down as I work, but don't comment—I know he's intentionally going to leave the delivery here for me so I can work on our project this evening.

He walks around the room, quizzically appraising everything as he searches for his younger sister's hiding spot. Hansel crosses an arm over his chest, grabbing his elbow as his free hand migrates toward his chin.

"Well, she's obviously not *in* the fireplace," he muses. His footsteps are heavy and intentional. "And I know you didn't move the fireplace—I measured after the last time. She's not in the loft. You hid her under the floorboards yesterday, so I'm guessing you wouldn't repeat that."

Hansel steps closer to me before reaching up to flick the long strands of my bangs back, smirking. I consider making it look like the fireplace has moved a foot while he's busy staring at me, but I don't.

"I can't help but notice the flour in your hair, mistress baker, might that be a clue?" His nose is an inch away from my ear, and I shudder as his breath ripples against my skin. Blinking, I try to keep my composure.

"A clue that I run a bakery? Why, *yes*, however did you guess?" My words are sickly sweet. His eyes spark with laughter.

"Where is she, Annika?" he whispers quietly.

"You can come out, Gretel," I call, refusing to give him her location.

The lid scrapes off the barrel. Hansel turns back toward the fireplace, dropping the strand of my hair he was twisting around his finger. His face lights up when Gretel appears.

"Well," he drawls. "There she is. Not bad, little sister. I never would have guessed."

"Not until you tried to move the barrel," I add.

"Oh, I don't know about that. Gretel's as heavy as a barrel of flour now." He offers his sister a hand as she smacks at him for his joke. At thirteen, Gretel is the resistance's best weapon.

"You realize I have to take her home, right?" Hansel teases. "I can't take her out of here looking like she just lost a fight with Winter."

He bends down and starts brushing the flour off of Gretel's dress. The barrel was mostly empty, but everywhere Gretel brushes against the sides of it, traces of the white fluff adhered itself to her clothing. I could create the illusion of her being clean and save some time, but it would only last until they got halfway home.

"See you tomorrow," Gretel says, waving as her brother herds her out the door.

"See you tomorrow, Annika," Hansel adds in a deep voice. He tosses a look back at me, and I know it won't be long before he returns for his bag.

Once they're gone, I scoop it up and paw through the contents. Hansel doesn't mind me going through his things, but somehow it always feels a little wrong, despite the fact that he's hidden pieces of our device inside his belongings for me.

I come up with an apple in my hand, a small ribbon tied around the stem. I try to bite back my grin, but he's not here to see me, so I allow myself this small moment as I twist his gift in my fingers.

Hansel and I have worked together for years, but our mission is too important to let our feelings get in the way of what we need to accomplish. Still, the last few weeks, Hansel hasn't seemed to care. I told him it was a bad idea last week when he kissed me…that hasn't stopped us from kissing again since. It's reckless, but I've always felt Hansel was meant for me.

"Not bad," I murmur, holding the hinge up to the light when I find it in his bag. It would fit perfectly inside of the compartment. I set to work installing it before night falls and it becomes harder to see.

A few hours go by before I hear Hansel knock. I set down the tools I'm using and walk to the door—

somehow this is easier when he just walks in to pick up Gretel—the formality of knocking sets me on edge. His grin does not.

"Did it work?" he asks, stepping into the shadows of the room. He scoops me into his arms, and I drop the hand I had poised to cast an illusion over the room to protect my work had it not been Hansel at the door. The moon is partially in the sky, though twilight still glitters above us.

"Seems like it." I motion toward the tall outline of a tiered cake.

Hansel's arms drag around me as he steps toward the fake pastry.

"Your father would be so proud, Annika." He tosses a look back at me. His muscles flex as he steps around the mobile hiding place I wheeled out of the back room to work on. "I know you never wanted to follow in his footsteps, but God himself had to plan to put you here in our time of need."

Hansel strides back over to me, wrapping his arms around my waist once again.

"The resistance would be lost without you, Annika. No one else has been able to get us this close to the king." The fate of our country somehow rests on two eighteen-year-olds and a thirteen-year-old-assassin.

Outside, the fireworks explode in the sky with streaks of white light. It illuminates the rooftops in the distance, round and sloping in candy-colored stripes. Walls glitter against the burst of light.

"Right on time," Hansel mumbles, leaning in to press his lips against mine.

"This joke is getting old, Hansel," I mumble, silently willing him not to stop kissing me. My breath catches as he pulls back.

"You would prefer I talk business during the display?" His smirk casts deep shadows over his face as the sky lights up again.

"I didn't say that," I mumble, his lips roaming over mine as his hands tangle in my hair. Brown locks slip from the loose bun on top of my head.

The tangy scent of apple hovers between us from the present he left me earlier, lingering on my lips as he separates them. All around us, candles grow brighter, intensifying as Hansel pushes me backward toward the table. I bump into it, dropping to sit on the workspace as I drag him down with me.

Hansel pulls back to grin, light dancing over his face as it grows even more golden. His hand reaches behind me, steadying himself as he leans back down to kiss me.

"You should learn to control that," I tease.

"You make me light up, what can I say, Annika?" His voice is low, and dangerous enough that my stomach twists up. "The lights only do what I tell them to do."

Fireworks crackle outside over the city, casting a

white glow over us for a moment, mixing with the golden gleam of the candles burning brightly enough to be a raging wildfire.

"And you think letting the king's guards know we're here is a good idea—they can probably see us from the city the way this place looks like it's ablaze."

Hansel's eyes crackle and spark like the flames around us, but he lowers his eyelids, forcing himself to consider my words.

"Fine." He sighs, dousing the lights until only two glow dimly off to the side. "Happy now, mistress baker?"

I was happier when he was kissing me, but I refuse to say it out loud.

"I'm happy that I don't have to whip up an illusion to keep the guards from noticing us," I pretend to chide, ducking under his arm as I slide away from the table.

"Annika," he calls quietly. A candle near me bursts.

I turn as he illuminates the fireplace again, the last of the fireworks fading in the sky outside the window. I wander back over to him but hover just out of reach.

Glancing up, I create a crystal chandelier above us. It picks up the firelight and glitters around the room.

"And here I thought *I* was going to be the one to get us caught." He smirks, revealing deep dimples on his cheeks.

"Well, I need something pretty to inspire me now that I can start working on the cake again. It's a good thing that hinge fits, Hansel."

"I know, but we have it now and we can move forward with our plans." He reaches forward and carefully wraps an arm around my waist as he turns me toward where I've hidden the wooden cake form.

"Is she ready?" I ask, waving my hand to unveil the cake. The cloak drops from around it like a sheet, the illusion wall disappearing before our eyes to reveal the cake.

"I hope so," Hansel whispers. "You'd know more than me. One more reason we'd be lost without you."

"Hansel, are *you* ready?" I ask cautiously. We've been preparing for this for what seems like an entire lifetime, but now that the time is drawing near, we're all a little terrified of what could go wrong.

"I'll save her," he whispers quietly, but his grimace is a silent admission that he's scared of what might happen.

"You will," I whisper back, wrapping my hand around his arm. Sometimes, he still flinches when I touch him, as if he's not expecting me to be so familiar with him, but he looks down to me, soft smile on his lips and lowers his face to me.

"She'll be all right," he says after a moment. "She's got both of us—we'll make sure she's safe."

"You'll pull her back, Hansel," I assure him. "We'll all make it through."

An explosion ripples outside. The entire house shakes under the weight of the blast. If the chandelier I created had been real, the glass would have clinked together and fallen to the floor, smashing into a million pieces. Instead, it's the only thing that doesn't move.

"What in the name of the king's court?" Hansel races to the window, ground still trembling.

"What do you see?" I ask, pausing just long enough to cover the room in an illusion to conceal our secret.

By the time I reach the window, smoke fills the air, dancing in the night. Hansel douses the lights so we can see outside without interference.

My hand feels cold as I place it along the window sill. The king must have had an enemy in our sister town, but instead of dealing with it discretely like he usually does, he took down what I estimate to be half the tiny town. Thankfully it's in the opposite direction that Hansel and Gretel's home is in, though I'm sure if they blew something up, the guards will also be making the rounds to look for others to destroy.

"How fast can you finish that cake, Annika?" Hansel's voice is dark. If he's willing to speed up the timeline like this, it must be worse than I think.

"What do you know about this, Hansel? What did you see today?"

Hansel spends his days traveling for work and has his ear to the ground more than any of us. Nothing happens in this country that he doesn't have a way of learning about.

"If it's who I think it is, it's not one of ours."

My eyes close in relief. I'm horrified that someone has died tonight, but at least it's not one of our own.

Hansel opens his mouth to speak, but I cut him off. "Gretel."

He pauses, jaw still open for the briefest of moments before he closes it and nods. Hansel pulls me close, kissing me hard.

"Be safe." His voice echoes in my head as he rushes to the door. Once outside, he spins and looks at me, demanding I cast an illusion.

Shaking my head to pull myself from the fog, I arch my hand, transforming the bakery into a rundown old building. The lights go out on the outside, leaving nothing but a shadowy old house that's about to fall apart. Only the window remains for him to see me.

Hansel nods, approving of my choice. Quickly, he ducks his head and turns away, running from the bakery toward Leipden where he left Gretel in the care of his great aunt.

I wave my hand again, concealing the window from the outside.

Inside, I throw strings of lights around the room, casting a white glow over my workspace. I tear down the illusion wall and reveal the cake form again so I can work —I won't be sleeping tonight.

The king must die, and my chandelier-lit handiwork

will be the trojan horse that leads to his death at the hands of a thirteen-year-old girl that acts as a guardian of death and life.

Hansel casts a worried look at me as he drops off Gretel the next morning. She rushes in, clearly having slept through the explosion—though she was farther away and it might not have made an impact in Leipden—and dances around the room.

As soon as Hansel is down the drive, Gretel drops her act.

"What happened?" she demands, taking me by surprise. "He didn't tell me, but it can't be good."

"An explosion," I answer. "That's as much as I know. I'm sure he'll learn more about it today."

"We need to move up the timeline," she replies. Her jaw twitches with nerves—something I've seen repeatedly over our time together.

"We can't exactly convince the king to change his party, Gretel," I remind her. "He's already sent word on what he wants for his cake. In a week, we'll deliver the one we made for you instead. We have to be patient, darling."

"A week and two days," Gretel murmurs, brushing back her long hair. *Of course* she would know the exact countdown—it's the day *she* might die as well. She drops her hand quickly, face hardening. "Can't we force his hand?"

"For a ball?" I scoff. "No, our plan is a good one, but we can't even suggest he move up his party or he will know something is wrong."

"I just want to get this over with." She's frustrated, and I can't blame her.

"We'll get you out of there, Gretel." My words are soft as I try to soothe her fears. "Hansel won't let anything bad happen to you."

"I'm killing the king of Candestrachen." She looks at me incredulously. "I'll do what I must."

Gretel has always been willing to sacrifice herself for the cause—better to give up a few lives and save the masses than to watch us all perish at the hands of a corrupt and unpredictable king—but Hansel and I are willing to do what we must to keep her alive. Besides, we might need her again for the next man who rises to power.

"They won't even know it's you, Gretel, I promise. You'll look like someone else entirely."

"If you can get in the door," she reminds me. Turning, she makes her way to the cake form.

"I have to bring the cake in. I'll find a way to be in the room, Gretel. I won't let you down. Once it's over, Hansel will pull you back and get you out of there."

"His lightness and my darkness," she muses.

"You have life and death, Gretel." I walk up behind her and take her long mane in my hands. Braiding it quietly, I add, "Hansel has light. He will pull you back from the darkness when you destroy King Levin. I know you don't like using death, but we're all grateful to you, Gretel."

She's quiet for a long time. I would be terrified if I were in her position. Entering the palace in a Trojan cake with the intent of killing the mad king—if anything goes off plan even in the slightest—there's no telling what the crown would do to a thirteen-year-old assassin.

"Will you at least give me brown hair like yours? And make me look older?" She places her request for an illusion to change her appearance while in the palace.

"Would you like my face too, Gretel?" I laugh.

"No, but only because they'd come after you afterward." She turns, and the braid falls from my hand.

"What's wrong with your hair, my little darling?" I prompt, hands on my hips. A smirk tugs at my lips but I try to hold it back.

"Nothing," she remarks, curving around me to walk along the wall toward the window. The girl touches a plant sitting there and it springs to life, bursting with flowers. "I just like yours better. Besides, if I'm going to look different, I should look *very* different."

"Fine, brunette it is. Now, do you intend on helping

today, or are you planning on frolicking around the bakery all day growing things?"

She turns to see what else she can sprout with her touch in the cool fall weather. Before she can notice, I create a few vines as an illusion a few feet away. Gretel moves to touch them, but she can't make them grow.

I flick my fingers by my side, changing the positions of the vines. My charge turns around to glare at me. "Very funny."

"I try." I don't bother hiding my grin this time.

"You and Hansel were made for each other." Gretel rolls her eyes. She doesn't know about us yet, but if we survive the assassination, we'll have to tell her.

"Well, what do you expect, little bird? We were raised by our fathers—they were practically like brothers, so of course, we have the same training."

"Yes, *that's* what I meant," she mumbles so low that I almost miss it. Perhaps she *does* have an idea of what's going on without her.

"Come along, Gretel. I've had enough of waiting around for answers. We're going to town for supplies."

"Hansel will be furious." That doesn't stop her. She grabs a cloak from the rack by the door and wraps it around her shoulders. Bright pink tones make her hair pop, and her eyes sparkle as she looks back at me.

I wrap a brilliant blue and lavender shawl around my shoulders, the long center corner hanging down my back.

The tassels tickle against my arms, but no matter what walk of life you are from, in the towns of Candestrachen, the women are meant to be seen in bright colors and ornate clothing.

My long skirt bounces around my ankles as I walk. It's a muted gray color—one that would be entirely unacceptable in town under normal circumstances, but it's best for baking in. When we finish walking through the woods, I'll use an illusion and make myself more presentable.

Gretel flicks her wrist and brings a blueberry bush back to life, fruit springing out of its branches. She pauses long enough to gather a handful of berries and pats the bush as if it were a dog. Holding her hand out, she offers me some.

I indulge, but only a few so she can have the rest. Gretel is about to save us all—she should have whatever her heart desires in the coming days.

Music swells up in the distance. Gretel sighs, displeased with the display we're too far away to see.

When we reach the edge of the tree line, I transform my dress into a brilliant gown that matches the cotton candy colors of the center of the town of Leipden. We round the corner and reach the true spectacle.

King Levin doesn't like for his people to work where he can see them. Anyone trapped inside of the city centers is forced to create a spectacle for the king and his guests to see, as if the entire country were one big festival. People like Hansel and I who live outside of the town limits were given permission to work, but the poor souls inside still had to provide for their families without any source of income—we help however we can, but it's still not enough.

Young men sometimes sneak out to live with relatives in the woods while the women stay behind to cover for them using their flashy dresses to catch the noblemen's eye in the streets as they bustle about, pretending to be happy. When Hansel and the others find the ones that escaped, they put them to work, giving them a place to belong and a way to help their families back in the towns.

Gretel falls behind me just slightly, her now-vibrant dress bouncing with each step. She stays behind my elbow as she follows me through the streets.

"Good morning, Annika," a voice calls. A friendly hand waves as the gentleman pushes a cart through the town. I wave back, offering a smile.

I make my way to the miller's shop to order more flour. While I have enough to last through the assassination attempt, I need to make it look like business as usual. The miller's shop is far enough away from the flour mill that I imagine it's difficult for Bauer to run his job, much less help lead the resistance.

The buildings loom over us, looking down on two young women making their way through the streets of

Leipden. Each tower on every building is striped with a different color, winding its way around the pointed precipice of the roofs.

Bold magentas and orange tones dot this section of the town, mixed with bright whites like a twisted mint. Perhaps it's unfair of me to compare everything here to a candy world, but when one's entire life revolves around baking and creating confectionary delights for royals and peasants alike, one has little else to compare the bright world too.

We pass a row of brightly designed fireworks meant for later this evening. I secretly wish Gretel's powers extended to turning inanimate objects into duds so we could have one night of peace in the skies.

Turning, I allow my hand to scrape over the embossed edges of the building at the start of the street. Each groove is familiar beneath my hands. From the corner of my eye, I see Gretel do the same.

A group of young girls runs by us, clad in bright yellows and blues. They spin, laughing as they run down the street. Their mothers have taught them to have fun with the king's little games, but when they're older, they'll learn the truth of their prison.

A bell dings above me as I guide my charge into the miller's shop. Bauer looks up from his place behind the counter, a streak of flour runs across one side of his forehead.

"Ahh, young Miss Annika and her apprentice," he regards us. "What can I help you ladies with today?"

"The King is coming!" someone shouts outside. Bauer tosses me a worried glance but hurries around the counter on his bad leg. Gretel and I pick up our skirts and step out of the door before the miller—I can't let the crown see our secret child-weapon.

CHAPTER 2

In the streets, people are busy lining the walkways, ready to put on a show for when the king passes by with whatever dignitaries he has hanging on his every word today.

Lights flicker on down the length of the street. Despite being trapped in Leipden, the people have developed a system over the years to help each other out. A lookout sounds the alarm when a member of the crown's guards come close. Lights are turned on only when necessary, and the people crowd into the streets. When possible, a few slip away into the darkened corners of a shop to be productive while they can.

Everything sparks to life as if we've all been in the streets celebrating all day. Men raise their glasses and women dance as voices fill the air with rehearsed lines.

I tuck Gretel behind me, using my tall frame to block her. Bauer sidles up next to me, leaning on my arm for support as he too covers Gretel from sight. He reaches up to swipe the flour from his face, jostling his light brown hair in the process.

The parade files past us, led by guards in brightly colored uniforms. Should anyone ever attack Candestrachen, there will be no hope for us—subtlety is not the king's strong suit and his guards are more easily spotted then the women's dresses.

A cart wheels by—Hansel would be fascinated by how they power it. A short man sits in the front, guiding it down the roads as an engine quietly hums beneath him. We don't have access to all of the technology the king has, but Hansel has ways of finding things we aren't supposed to have.

A woman in royal blue raises the shout, and we all follow, watching the vehicle move.

"A blessing to King Levin and to Candestrachen!"

When the third round of cheers dies down, the king leans out of the red, white, and yellow cart. He waves his hand, tousling his dark brown hair—if I didn't know any better, I'd say we could be twins…if I were a decade and a half older, that is.

Music fills the air as musicians dive into song—it doesn't matter which one. A group of older women starts singing, swaying together in unison. I raise my voice with them, knowing I need to blend in as I croon about the magnificence of Candestrachen. Gretel sings behind me but stays hidden.

The king eyes us all as he passes by, a calculated, jovial grin on his face as he points us out to the man seated next to him. The lights on the miller's shop behind me flicker in bursts of bright colors, painting light over King Levin's face—his father before him was handsome, and one could even argue that Levin was a sight, but the blood on his hands has stripped away every last shred of humanity I could ever find in him.

He locks eyes with me for a moment, focusing on my face. My muscles go stiff with the shock of his gaze but I force myself to smile, and I sing—his death is coming, and I will be glad for it.

"You know what color we're missing here?" The king shouts to his companion. I hold my breath, knowing what's coming. "Red!"

The cart wheels down the street and around a corner. Terrified, people run around buildings hoping to catch him on the other side—if they're in his presence, they're safe.

Several guards in the back stop, prepared to carry out

his coded orders. We didn't put on enough of a show for his guest, and one of us will pay the price.

"Go," I murmur, pushing Gretel back toward the door. I step back, not turning away from the street, trying not to draw attention to our escape.

Bauer grasps at Gretel, catching my arm by mistake. Four, five, six steps and we're at the door to the shop, and he pushes us in, closing it behind us.

The street erupts in our wake as men and women try to avoid the guards—whomever they catch first will be the one to add red blood to the streets. Stifled screams fill the air—it will be worse if the king hears our cries from the next street over—but those near the guards can't help but call out in fear.

"Annika!" Bauer tries to keep his voice down as he shouts at me.

I wheel around to find him pointing to a hidden compartment in the wall. I suppose I don't need to find a place to hide Gretel after all.

"You too," he hisses, grabbing my arm to force me into the compartment. I start to argue, but I know he's right. For as much as the resistance needs Gretel, they need me too—at least until next week. "I'll be fine."

Once inside, the panel slides shut, concealing us from view. Through a small hole, I can see Bauer hiding behind his counter, ready to act as if he were the only person hiding in the miller's shop should the guards choose his establishment to disrupt.

I add a secondary wall in front of ours, preventing the guards from finding the secret panel, should any of them be smart enough to look.

"*Don't,*" Bauer warns when he notices. I drop my hand, taking his advice not to hide him—if anyone saw us come in and they don't find anyone, they'll tear the shop apart and find us all.

We all have to make sacrifices for the cause.

Gretel presses up against me, also trying to see through the small hole. I wave my hand and add a second one to allow her to see what I see.

Minutes pass by. The waiting is the hardest part—possibly even harder than the small pop we hear five minutes later. Somewhere, someone has been tied to posts with a small explosive device attached to them, only big enough to tear them apart when it goes off. Blood is splattered, coating the area red as onlookers cry tears of sorrow and relief. Soon, somewhere new will be painted red with the blood pooling on the ground as the guards finish their assignment.

I drop the illusion, and Bauer releases us from the small hole in the wall. I climb out, pushing and pulling my skirt into place as I stand. Worried, I quickly change the colors and styles of our dresses before we leave the miller's shop.

"What do we know?" I ask, trying not to sound shaken. I smooth back my hair, knowing at least part of it has toppled out of its bun.

"The explosion last night?" Bauer asks. "Not much, I'm afraid. I was waiting for Hansel to come tell me. I'm afraid we have much to worry about, though."

He loops around to stand behind his counter, as if ready to take my order. I lean forward onto the countertop as he scribbles on a pad.

"Are you ready?" he asks, head still down.

"We will be."

"I'm ready," Gretel chimes in, furious over the events of the morning. "He will pay for this."

"Gretel, this is not a mission of revenge," Bauer snaps. "If that is why you are doing this, I'll pull you out right now. We are preventing further loss of life; that is all."

"Yes, Bauer. I know. I'm sorry," Gretel hangs her head. "It is for the greater good—for the future lives."

"We can't change the past," Bauer concludes. "You *will* save the future, though, Gretel."

He swings back to me, dropping the conversation. Gretel may be the key to stopping the king, but she's still a child, and it amazes me how some of the resistance treat her as one.

"Take her home, Annika, and do not come back here until it's time for the delivery," he instructs. His implication is clear—I messed up by bringing her out this close to the assassination attempt.

Bauer hands me a bag of flour, softening his gaze. One side of his lips tick up—an apology for being harsh. I take the flour from him and hand it to Gretel before resting a second bag on my hip.

The streets are back to bustling when we exit the shop. Gretel's green dress is a startling difference to the pink one I had created for her earlier, but I need her to look drastically different. I'm not sure if the king will remember me when I journey to the palace next week, but I certainly hope not. I'd change my hair if I could, but enough people know I'm the baker that if I showed up without my signature brown locks, they'd know something was wrong.

Music trickles its way down the streets, calling for us to join the celebration, but we avoid it. Instead, we follow the main street laid with colorful rocks until we can turn onto a side road that leads back to the woods. Gretel knows to keep quiet until we enter the trees, but I purposely take the long way, knowing we won't run into the remnants of whatever poor soul painted the town red this morning.

"Are you okay?" I ask as soon as we are concealed in the tree line.

The illusions drop around us, and we stand in our

muted clothing again, the only signs of color left back on the town rooftops that peer through the tops of the trees.

"Bauer seemed angry," she comments.

"Bauer is always angry."

"Not with Hansel," Gretel corrects.

"That's because *Hansel* plays by the rules," I remind her.

Gretel stomps off, leaving me to trail behind her. The trees rustle on the wind and Gretel waves her hand, leaving a trail of bright green leaves where dying ones had once clung.

A gasp stops us.

Turning to the right, I search the bushes for the source of it. Throwing my hand out, I add illusion leaves to the ones Gretel gave new life to, creating a wall of greenery between us and the voice, as if the wind had blown them to cover their sight.

His uniform is green, covered in designs of white, cream, and yellow—the guard nearly blends in with the foliage. He staggers back, eyes wide.

"You're a witch; a magic woman." He collides with a tree.

"Whatever are you talking about?" I adopt a fake cheery tone as he takes in my altered appearance—an old, haggard woman. "Are you all right, sir. When we found you, you looked like you had hit your head."

"Don't approach me, woman!" His hands claw around the back of the tree as if he wants to pull it out by the roots and throw it at me. "Your kind has been banished for decades—they don't exist here anymore."

"Sir, I don't know what you're talking about." Another step toward him and the apprehension on his face slips away. He grasps his weapon and aims it at me.

"No!" A scream tears from Gretel's lips. She throws herself on the ground behind me, her hand stretching out just far enough for me to see in my peripheral vision, and the entire forest twists.

Trees burst from the ground, while others rearrange themselves, moving from the roots. Vines drop from branches, while bushes spring up around our feet. A wall of massive trees separates us from the guard.

Instead of fighting to reach me around the bark, he turns and runs toward the town. We're in trouble.

"Gretel, change the forest," I instruct. I drop my illusions as she grows new paths all around us, changing the way to the bakery to make it nearly impossible to find.

"He'll go to the king about this," Gretel says from her place on the ground. She summons more plant life, hindering the man's way back to the palace.

"We need to get back, Gretel, hurry."

I scoop up the bags of flour we both dropped and pull her off the ground. I start running, but with the changed landscape, I'm not even sure we're headed in the right direction.

The ripple effect travels before us, the forest quietly changing as Gretel's summons moves throughout the woods. I slam to a halt as a new tree presents itself in our path. Turning, I pull the little girl around it, taking a different route.

I hear the voices before I see them—men.

"Do you have any idea where to go?" one asks.

"This isn't right, the path should be right here."

"Are you drunk, my friend—spent too much time out last night?" a third calls jovially, enjoying the confusion. He slaps the second man on the shoulder loudly. Perhaps *he* is the one who spent too much time out last night.

"Something isn't right." I recognize the fourth voice—Hansel. This must be his team. Then I realize I know the other voices as well.

"Hansel!" I shout as we step around the tree blocking our view.

His head whips around to me. All of the boys are carrying large sacks on their shoulders. Pickaxes and other tools are attached to the belts on their waists. Hansel's eyes widen as he takes me in.

He stalks over to me, grabbing my elbow to spin me.

"Get us home, Hansel," I whisper before he can speak.

"You did this?" He looks to Gretel.

"Get us to the bakery," I demand again, knowing we can explain later.

"Boys, we're officially off duty. Come on," Hansel calls, waving them over.

His team surrounds us, and we set off in the direction we believe the bakery to be in. Gretel's ripple slows, transitioning quietly into the world we know as we get close to the bakery.

Hansel's feet pound into the ground alongside of me, clearly frustrated as I quietly explain what happened. The muscles in his arm are stiff as I collide with them as we walk.

The bakery is a tall, two-story building with high ceilings downstairs, perfect for creating my confections. The dark brown tones of the wood are highlighted by pops of aqua blue and cream, my father's homage to my late mother. Whereas the towns are covered in decadent architecture, out in the woods, we are more understated with our buildings, only adding color at the king's demand.

Hansel takes the stairs two at a time and Gretel, and I struggle to keep up. The team of six waits outside, watching for anyone who might be coming our way.

I wave Gretel off as I follow Hansel to the back wall near the stairs. The little girl mills by the fireplace as I create an illusion wall between us, shortening the interior of the house by ten feet.

Anger rolls off Hansel in waves, and as I turn, his face softens with worry before slamming me into the back wall. His arms go around me protectively, caressing my waist while his lips move against mine—not the conversation I was expecting to have, but I much prefer it.

"Are you okay?" His lips catch on mine as he tries to speak between kisses.

"Yes," I mumble, words catching against his skin.

One hand quickly reaches into my hair, working his fingers between the strands. I wrap myself around him, holding his back with one hand, the other palm cradling the back of his head just above his neck.

I can hardly breathe as he crushes against me, worry written on his face as he pulls back with a wrinkled brow.

"What were you thinking?" he whispers harshly, chest dragging up and down against me as he struggles to catch his breath.

"I was ordering flour from Bauer," I protest. I run my hand along his arm, hoping to soothe him. "I was trying to keep up appearances. I knew I'd need next week to finish the cake form, and we need to create all of the pastries for our cover story before that happens."

Hansel tips his head forward to learn against my forehead.

"Annika, what would have happened if we had lost you?"

"Bauer and I were going to protect Gretel."

"Yes, but I'm asking about *you*." His hand twists in my hair that is now fully released from the bun I had wound it in. It cascades down behind me, tumbling to the sides.

I pull him toward me, pressing his chest against me as he cocoons us against the wall. His sister is only a few feet away on the other side of my magical wall, and his team is only on the other side of the door, but I don't care—neither does he. His voice is hushed as he speaks, but actions are louder than any words and Hansel's movements are saying a great deal.

My back moves away from the wall as I lean forward to kiss him, our lips colliding and parting furiously. His arms reach around me and for a moment, I think he might pick me up and carry me away to a safer town far away from Candrestrachen. My fingers slip around his suspenders, and I'm careful not to let them snap out of my fingers as I pull him closer. He grins against me, laughing so quietly that it flutters over my skin.

"I will not lose you, Annika," he responds to his own question. "You're too important to the cause and too important to Gretel and me."

"You'll be just fine without me if it ever comes to it." I sigh—if I could stay hidden behind this wall with the people I care about for the rest of my life out of the sight of the king, I'd be happy.

His hand comes up to my chin, tipping my face up to

look at him. His eyes are intently focused on me as I gulp air. His shoulders sag with each breath, and I realize we should have pulled apart earlier.

"Don't sugarcoat this, Annika. We can't lose you." Hansel is frustrated, but I don't back down.

"I'm a baker—sugarcoating is what I do, or haven't you ever tried my palmiers?" I snap back. I regret bringing his favorite dessert into the conversation, but I'm not going to tolerate him saying I'm being too soft about this. I'm not the important one here—the focus should be entirely on Gretel.

I should bake him something later as an apology— maybe my peanut butter fudge that he loves so much.

"We have to go back out there," I inform him. I'd pull away if I could, but he still has me trapped against the wall.

"Is Gretel okay?" he asks reluctantly. As he takes his arms from around me, I realized he's had me up on my tiptoes this entire time, supporting part of my weight as we kissed. I feel heavy without him holding me up.

"I think she's scared about all this, but she's not wavering."

"What about the woods?"

"The guard scared her—she reacted out of fear. She did the right thing changing the forest, but I think upending everything like that unnerved her a little."

"It will be easier when she only has one task to focus on and not changing an entire landscape."

"Speaking of, how are the locals going to get around now?"

"Most of them stay out of the woods, so it's really just our teams," Hansel says, thinking it through. "I'll come up with a signal so we know how to find our way back here."

I nod, trusting him to handle the situation. Hansel has always been a problem solver.

"Annika, I think Gretel needs to stay with you until this is over. We can't risk her traveling now that we're so close."

"You don't think they'll notice you traveling without her? We can't afford questions. They'll notice you coming and going without her even if you *don't* live in town."

His hand grazes mine, fingers wrapping around mine slowly before pulling away. Hansel holds my gaze and brushes back a strand of hair. I tip my head toward him and rub the back of his hand with my cheek.

He sighs and pulls away. Reaching up, I wrap my hair back into a loose bun making him smile.

"I'm going to make a trail of lights," he informs me, stepping back. I follow him.

"They won't notice that?"

"Blinking lights," he corrects. "Electronic fireflies. They won't have any idea."

I consider the merits of his idea. If he creates a path of

tiny devices that flicker like an insect, people who pass by won't know. No one will stand for prolonged periods of time to watch for a trail, nor is it uncommon for an insect to land on a bush and stay there for a time. It makes sense. If anyone can get access to technology for that, it's my co-conspirator.

"That's brilliant, Hansel."

"I save all my best ideas for you and the mission, Annika," he teases. "Gretel will stay here with you tonight —don't argue. I'll take her home tomorrow after I set the trail in place."

"You mean *after* you figure out how to get home." His back is turned to me, but his head twitches to the side as if he started to turn back to me.

"Another reason she's spending the night here—I don't know how to get her home safely yet. Just start your baking project early since you'll have the extra help. It will cover for us in case things get busy over the next few days and you can't make your stockpile supply to use as a cover."

Hansel nearly walks into the illusion wall, trusting me to take it down in time. If I didn't want to kiss him again soon, I'd let him walk into it, but I need his face to stay intact if I want to taste his lips again. I wave my hand and the wall drops as he raises his voice.

"We have a plan," he announces, brushing back his hair. I hope my own mane looks all right—he would have told me if it hadn't because he doesn't want to give away our secret any more than I do.

Gretel turns, jaw locked. Two of Hansel's team members stand in the bakery, looking annoyed. One uncrosses his arms, letting them fall to his side while the other raises an eyebrow.

"What exactly is this plan?" asks the one who was clearly just pretending to be drunk. Aurik has always been unique.

"We're marking the trails tonight, boys. We'll come back tomorrow. Annika will be babysitting."

"What?" Gretel shrieks.

Hansel motions for the guys to leave the bakery and they oblige, turning on the heels of their work boots. They leave bits of dried mud in their wake for me to sweep later.

Few people know Gretel is the key to the rebellion's success—it's too dangerous for people to know. As far as most people are concerned, Gretel is just Hansel's kid sister and responsibility since his father died. Aurik and Brahms know, but even so, some distance is kept.

The fierce little girl marches up to her brother, not letting on how tired she must be after rearranging an entire forest.

"Why am I being left here?" Her long blonde bangs fall in front of her face, and she pushes them back harshly.

"I don't know how to get home, which means it's not

safe to take you out. Annika needs your help tonight anyway to work on the food supply for your alibi. I have a feeling next week won't be kind to us."

"Hansel has to concentrate on building firefly bots anyway," I inform her, touching her elbow softly. "He's going to light the paths so we can find each other."

"Just do what Annika says," Hansel directs his sister. He hugs her quickly, tossing a glance at me. He mouths, "Sugarcoat it."

He eyes his sister before he pulls away—she doesn't need to know how difficult her handiwork has just made our lives.

Hansel is worried, and I don't blame him. So much could go wrong over the next few days.

"They won't even think to look here, Hansel," I promise. "It will be safe."

I twirl my hand in the air, coating the entire outside of the bakery in bright colors. Hansel laughs from the drive outside when he turns to see my handiwork, the team members mercifully already in the woods. Sculptures of candy wrap around the columns of the porch—everything Hansel's sweet tooth has ever craved over the years. The top of the bakery now has points like the buildings in the cities—mine drenched in what looks like whipped cream and pink frosting. Chocolate drips from the shutters coated in rainbow colored sprinkles found in only one shop in the entire kingdom. The door is covered in melted green and white peppermint, leaving the steps transformed into rows of salt water taffy lined with lollipops.

I've sugarcoated the world for Hansel and Gretel...at least for now.

"Could you flirt any harder?" Gretel mumbles next to me once her brother is out of sight. I whip around to face her. "I'm about to kill a king, Annika, you think I don't notice the things around me? Conjuring up all of Hansel's favorite sweets was a clear and definite message to him. Now, take it down before anyone else sees."

"Just for that..." I reply. Instead of finishing, I transform the interior of the bakery into a candy wonderland. The banister on the stairs twists into swirled rainbow candy canes, and a lavish sculpture protrudes from the wall with every treat imaginable. A chocolate fountain streams in the corner surrounded by a base of butterscotch candies. Macaroons and truffles line the fireplace mantle.

"I'll forgive you," she replies, "but only because I love macaroons and I know you have some real ones in the back."

I smile, leading the way after making sure the door lock is secure. She glides behind me gracefully—she'll be a force to be reckoned with when she grows up.

"We've got fudge to make tonight, Gretel."

"Oh lovely, more bribes for my brother."

"*You* like it, too," I remind her, tugging on a few strands of her hair. "We've got a lot to create tonight, so I hope you aren't tired."

"Considering we haven't had lunch yet, I guess we're in for a long day."

CHAPTER 3

A rock clicks against my window, waking me. The floor is cold as I set my feet down—the fire must have gone out downstairs. I've only been asleep for two hours, so it shouldn't have gone out so quickly, but perhaps the draft quieted the flames.

I reach for my cloak, tucking the hood up over my hair to help with the chill. A few long strands of hair tumble out from behind the fabric and I don't bother to tuck them back.

Hansel is standing below the window, poised to throw another pebble. I rest my hand on the window, and he drops his arm, knowing I've seen him.

I hurry down the stairs to let him in. The embers from the fire still glow in the blue-toned night. Only the moonlight illuminates the house now.

"You kept the candy, I see." He greets me with a smirk as he brushes past me to come inside.

"Only for you, Hansel."

"Where is Gretel?"

"She's still sleeping," I reply, closing the door.

"I'm here." Her tiny voice bounces off the walls in the early morning hours. She glides off the stairs, also wrapped in a cloak.

Hansel moves his hand, and the fire ignites once more. Another flick of his wrist and the candle bursts into flames too. A small light on the side of the room comes on, allowing us to see more easily.

He eyes me as if to say, *you really should watch that*, but I'm in no mood for his judgments. Hansel's gaze sweeps over to Gretel. Catching sight of the mountains of pastries we baked in the hours since Hansel left us, his eyes grow wide. Tarts and scones fill the table where we left them to cool. A few extra pies sit on the stools, though the rest are in the back. Cookies sit in baskets on an open rack off to the side, while rolls and sticky buns rest in containers waiting to be moved—we were too tired to transport everything into the back when we went to bed at two.

"Did you get everything done?" He asks, looking at Gretel.

"Mostly," I answer.

"Good." He nods, all business. "We need to go."

"It's four in the morning," Gretel complains, yawning. "You couldn't have just left us until morning?"

"No, Gretel, I couldn't." Dark shadows pass over Hansel's face. "The king's men are out looking for the witch that transformed the woods. If they found you here out of place, you both would have been detained for questioning. You and I have to go home *now* before they discover we aren't there."

Gretel's face pales in the candlelight. Hansel turns to me and scoops up one of my hands.

"You need to remove the illusion."

Startled, I raise my hand in an arc, dropping the façade outside. I had already removed it from the interior of the house as we worked because we needed more space to set the things we were baking. Hansel squeezes my hand before dropping it.

"Shoes, Gretel." He nods to his little sister's feet. She turns, rushing back upstairs to collect her things.

"Will you be all right here alone, Annika?" It's sweet that he's concerned.

"I have to be," I reply. I don't have a choice. "Will you two be okay out there?"

I'm terrified the king's men will find them as they

make their way back to Leipden. Their poor aunt must be beside herself.

"The course has changed, Annika, but there are still ways to get to and from the palace when this is all over. I know the way to you—I've lit the path. But here—" he holds out his hand, waiting for me to open mine, "—use these wisely. They're bots. They'll follow you wherever you go."

Tiny yellow lights blink in my hands, the same size as a firefly. I close my fingers around them.

"Once you activate them, they'll hover every hundred feet on their own until you run out. If you run out, they're programmed to move on their own, spacing themselves out further. If anything happens, Annika, and you need to run, these will let me find you."

Hansel is brilliant. I shouldn't be so shocked.

"Yours are yellow—I figured that would be the least likely to be noticed aside from the green ones I made for Gretel. Mine are a light blue."

"You had time to create these *and* mark the trails?" I ask skeptically.

"Well, *some* of the trails. This was more important." Hansel shakes his head, tossing his blond locks. "It appears some of Gretel's force is still at work and occasionally the boys have witnessed a tree moving. Most of it is farther out, mind you, but these were the only way to find each other if we have to."

"Oh, great," Gretel mutters, coming down the stairs. "I can't even handle an escape plan—are you *sure* I'm going to be able to kill the king?"

"You'll be fine," we both protest at the same time.

Gretel yawns again, fighting against only getting two hours of sleep. I like to think I'll be able to crawl back into bed once they're gone, but I know I'll be wide awake, worrying.

"You know the way home?" she asks.

"Yes, we just follow the blue trail." Hansel waves for me to follow them out into the yard. I slip on a pair of dainty slippers before stepping out onto the porch.

The grass is wet with early morning dew. Mixed with the cool weather, it soaks through my slippers, piercing my skin painfully. I'm grateful Gretel has boots on for the walk home.

"This way," Hansel says, leading us to a tree.

I wince as I follow behind them—I despise the cold weather, even when it hasn't fully arrived yet.

"See that little dot there?" Hansel points. I watch for a moment, seeing nothing. Then, a tiny blue glow appears down the path. A few seconds later, another blue dot glows so far away that I can barely see it. "That, ladies, is what you're looking for."

He takes a firefly from Gretel and shows us how to activate it. He has Gretel test it out, walking back toward the house. Once she reaches the porch, she returns to us, several lights still in her hand. Hansel demonstrates how to call the robotic creatures back to us before wrapping his arm around his little sister.

"Stay safe," he warns me. "Gretel and I will be back in a few hours."

I nod, waiting for them to leave but Hansel refuses to move until I'm standing in my doorway once again. When they slip out of sight, I lock the door.

Knowing it's a waste of my time to try to sleep, I set to work hiding the evidence of how Gretel and I spent the last twenty-four hours.

The sun is up, glistening off of the rooftops in the distance when Hansel and Gretel return. They're dressed brightly—Gretel bound in a deep red dress with laces up the front, and a navy cloak wrapped around her shoulders and Hansel outfitted in three different hues of dark green.

I noticed them through the window as they exited the woods, but look up when they knock, keeping to our usual routine in case anyone is watching. When planning to assassinate a king, paranoia is called preparedness.

"Good morning," I greet them, brushing back part of my hair. I feel woefully underdressed standing next to them. "What's all this?"

"The king's guard was out in full force this morning." Hansel's voice is deeper than usual as he drags a hand down his face. "You should change, too, in case they come this way."

My shoulders sag, but I move my hand out to transform my wardrobe into an illusion to match theirs.

"No, Annika. Change for real. You may need to hold other illusions in place should anything else happen."

I grimace—with an illusion, I can get dirty while baking without ruining my fancy clothes, but if I use real fabric, anything I drop onto it could be damaged. Crossing his arms, Hansel doesn't take no for an answer.

Gretel moves about the room, preparing for work as I turn and make my way to the stairs. If I have to be put out, I'm going to make a point of it.

My parent's room is large. When I first moved into it last year, I didn't know how to handle all the extra space, but I had wanted to be close to them and this was the only way I could think of to do it. Of course, as the new owner of the bakery, it was also expected, and should any of the king's guards ever inspect the house, there would be far too many questions raised if I was still in my childhood room.

I slip into a dusty pink dress, draping a light-colored fur over my shoulders. Pulling my necklace out from the collar of the dress, I let it rest on my chest as I navigate toward the stairs again. Hansel's eyes widen when he sees me.

"The ball is *next* week, Annika," Gretel jokes, snickering.

"Yes, but who doesn't like baking in furs, darling?" I retort, shaking my head playfully.

"I didn't mean you had to dress for town, Annika," Hansel adds, shaking his head.

"You made a good point, Hansel—we don't know what might happen later today, especially once the king starts to investigate the forest. Anyone could stop by."

"And *you* were being snarky," he muses, smirking.

"Of course." I wave him off. "Go to work, Hansel, something tells me you're going to be busy today."

Hansel angles himself toward the door, walking slowly. "Keep an eye out for the boys today."

I nod. If any of Hansel's team shows up today, it means something bad is happening. If he's worried enough to tell us to actively watch for them, we'd better be extra vigilant.

"Well, that's new," Hansel says from the door, looking out from under the porch. Gretel and I scurry over to look out of the doorway with him.

In the distance, nearly blocked out by the blinding light of the still-rising sun, something floats in the air. First one, then five, then enough that it could be a cloud if it weren't for the sun piercing through them, destroying the illusion.

"Are those…lanterns?" Gretel asks, squinting to see.

"Those are definitely lanterns," Hansel responds. His hand quietly bumps into mine.

"But those aren't ever sent up until night when the people can see them," Gretel whispers, realizing something is off.

"Stay in the house today." Hansel frowns, moving toward the steps.

"Wait," I call, turning to run back into the bakery. I hear Gretel say something to her brother as I pick up a small bag of the peanut butter fudge we made for Hansel last night. She brushes past me as I hurry onto the porch again.

Hansel raises an eyebrow, quirking one side of his lips up. He runs a hand through his hair as I approach him.

"I forgot to give this to you earlier." I hand him the candy.

"I give you apples, you give me fudge," he muses.

"We all have our different kinds of sweets, Hansel."

"Just like we all have our different kinds of gifts," he teases, finishing my thought. "But not all of us have those."

"Not all of us have sweets, either," I remind him quietly. "Don't let those go to waste."

"These won't even make it down the path, Annika,

and you know it." He grins, untying the ribbon holding the bag closed. "You spoil me, woman."

Hansel hands me the ribbon that matches my dress. I close my fingers around it, unsure of what to do with Gretel a few feet away in the house, likely watching through a window.

"Be careful, Annika. We don't know what's happening out there anymore. If you think anything is going wrong, get Gretel out of here and I'll find you." He pauses a moment before sighing. With a quick glance to the house, he turns and saunters off toward the woods.

Back inside, I set the ribbon down on the table. Draping the fur over the back of a chair, I instruct Gretel to sit by the window behind the curtains and watch for anyone coming from the woods. I'm less worried about the morning lanterns for the moment than I am for possible intruders.

I turn my attention to the wooden cake frame while Gretel keeps watch. I carve an intricate design into the wood for when I place the fondant over it—it will save me time on the design later. The wood scrapes under my knife, filling the room.

Gretel sighs loudly, nearly making me jump.

"Bored?" I ask playfully. I reach up and brush a piece of hair out of my face with the back of my wrist.

"How is the cake going?" she asks in a monotone voice to make her point. I giggle quietly.

"Well, they won't know it's not some elaborate sugar creation until after the fact," I reply. "Honestly, I'd like to get the fondant on and just get going with this."

I look up in time to see her cringe and realize I shouldn't wish the assassination—and her possible death —to come faster.

"Annika." Gretel's sharp voice tells me she hadn't been reacting to my comment.

"What is it?" I drop the tools I was using, flick my wrist to put an illusion over the half of the room where the wooden cake sits, and rush to her side.

"Bauer," Gretel murmurs. "This can't be good."

It feels like my internal organs drop inside of me like when I jumped off that cliff into the river as a child before King Levin took power. Air fills my mouth as I remember to breathe, gulping in oxygen.

"Go to the back, Gretel. Get the cake and go." I drop the illusion so the girl can move our secret weapon out of sight. The wheels drag against the floor as she pushes it away.

I rush to the door, opening it as Bauer hobbles up. He clutches at the neckline of his coat that falls below his knees. Stone blue makes his dark hair stand out.

"Bauer?"

He thrusts two large bags of flour at me. I fumble to catch them before they hit the ground. Straightening, I follow him inside, flour bags in my hands. Setting them on the table, I wait for his gasping to stop.

"What's happening?" My voice sounds hollow even to me.

Bauer starts to shake, breathing deeply. As he leans back, I flick my wrist toward him, rolling my fingers gently as if I were shooing a fly away from a freshly baked roll. A tall stool materializes behind him, catching him as he sits.

"Has anyone been here today?" he asks.

"No, just Hansel and Gretel."

"Where is she?" Bauer's brown locks fall in his face. Soft wrinkles form around his eyes and crease his brow from years of wear.

I nod to the back. Gretel steps out.

"We have to go," Bauer informs us, standing to his feet. His voice loses its wavering tone. Was this an act?

"Those lanterns were the start of something, girls, something bad."

"You're not really suggesting we leave, are you?" I ask, horrified.

"We can't leave you where they can find you," Bauer protests, looking less winded.

"What is going on, Bauer?" Gretel asks, crossing her arms over her chest. "We can't leave. If we do, how will we get me into the cake and delivered to the palace? Annika can't just abandon the bakery."

"What about the cake?" I ask, glancing at the back wall.

"Hansel and I will come back for it, but if anything happens to Gretel, all is lost. We can always come up with a new plan, but not without the girl," he confronts me. "We need to get you both somewhere safe."

"Where is that?" I demand, hands on my hips. I know Bauer would never move us without a reason and if he's willing to risk this plan, he must be exceptionally worried.

"Closer to the palace."

"Excuse me?"

"What?" Gretel speaks over me. "We can't be there until the ball. It's still days away."

"The king's guards will be scouring the towns, we can't move closer. Our ticket in is the cake—we have to wait until we take it to the palace for the ball." I frown.

"The guards aren't going to know who is bringing the king his cake, nor will they know where the baker appeared from. As long as *you* show up with the cake, everything will be fine, Annika." He puts his hand on my back and turns me toward the door.

"What do you know that we don't, Bauer?"

He sighs but continues to push at my back, propelling me forward.

"The king is searching for us. He's looking for rebels. Somehow, word has been spreading that a plan is to be enacted before the ball—rumors, as far as I can tell, I don't think we have a traitor—but he's scouring the cities looking for us…for *you* and for *her.*

"He's already searched the towns around the palace, and his men are branching out. If we can get you safely beyond the perimeter as it comes toward us, you'll be safe until they've completed their search."

"And if they find the bakery empty?"

"They won't, Annika, we'll make sure one of us is here. The guards don't know better unless they grew up here and knew your father. Even then, we should be able to explain it away. We just need to make sure you two are in the palace district."

Gretel looks nervously at me as we step outside and Bauer closes the door behind us. "We need to go."

I trust Bauer almost as much as I trust Hansel, so I swallow back my argument and take the steps down to the dirt path. The trees seem to swallow us as we step into the woods that are now completely unfamiliar to me.

A bird chirps loud enough to make Gretel jump, and she moves closer to me as we walk. Bauer limps along beside us at what must be a brutal pace for him, but he doesn't stop.

"Does Hansel know about this?" I ask.

"Not yet, but he will as soon as you're safe. Our next mission will be to rescue the cake."

I tap the fireflies to life, and the first takes its place to guide Hansel to find us—I won't risk him losing us should something happen along the way. Gretel notices me and nods.

"The lanterns this morning were some kind of signal, weren't they?" I question as the trees block out more of the light. Each leaf rattles as the wind picks up enough to blow my hair in front of my face. Reaching up, I pull it from the messy bun I'm wearing so that it falls to help prevent me from getting chilled.

"I'm afraid that was my fault," Bauer admits. "I was on my way from the mill to the shop and I saw the guards. I overheard their plan and knew I needed a way to get some attention.

"Our people all saw it—anything out of the ordinary makes them vigilant—but it also kept the guards distracted long enough to make it to a few of our key players to warn them. I came straight here as soon as I could find a way to escape without being noticed rushing from the town.

"Quiet now, girls," Bauer warns us, suddenly sensing something. He stops walking, straightening both of his knees. Dropping his voice, he adds, "We need to run."

CHAPTER 4

Grabbing Gretel's hand, Bauer launches forward, no longer limping—yet another of his façades. We crash through the bush, nearly colliding with a tree we forgot had recently moved.

Everything blurs around us as we stumble over the underbrush. My foot catches on a tree root, nearly sending me toppling forward. Gretel's long, blonde hair trails behind her as she leaps nimbly over tree roots and fallen branches.

Behind us, I hear the guards' voices calling to each other. After a moment, they catch the noise we're creating as we trample through the woods in the distance and follow us, quickly gaining speed.

"*Gretel,*" I call. She reaches for my hand so I can steady her as we run.

"Are you sure?" Bauer asks, wrenching himself around so he can assess our enemy.

"Is it her?" a guard yells.

"Do you honestly think a witch can run that fast?" another calls in reply.

"Oh, well, this is lovely," I grumble. "Time to give them a witch."

Gretel drags her hand across the rough bark of a tree as we pass by it. I'm sure it hurt, but she doesn't cry out. We pass another, and she darts her hand out again. The tree immediately begins to move, and I catch it from the corner of my eye as I pass it.

Unlike the last time, Gretel isn't transforming the forest. Her touch is merely coercing the trees to form a wall behind us, corralling the king's men away from us.

A firefly leaps from its place on the small pouch attached to my belt and darts toward the bushes. It blinks once before it disappears behind a bush left untouched by Gretel's commands.

I consider telling her to touch the ground and affect the roots of all the plants in the forest again, but Hansel and the others have already worked so hard to navigate the trails—it will be hard enough for him to locate us now and the line of trees is giving us a temporary reprieve from the chase. Still, we don't slow.

A bird cries out in shock as Gretel removes her hand from the bark of the tree it's sitting on. It flies into the air, lecturing her for disturbing its rest.

"Hurry, girls, we have to get to the town." Bauer pulls ahead of us, leading the way now that he's certain the trees are slowing the guards down. In the distance, I hear calls for the witch's head.

Gretel is breathing heavily, and I slow our pace. Bauer realizes we're lagging and slows as well, knowing we can't tax the girl before her mission. Each time she uses her gift, she depletes some of her power until she can recharge. Small tasks like bringing dying plants back to life in the bakery hardly affects her but rearranging an entire forest and now creating a wall of trees within two days will certainly take its toll on her—I can't let her do anything else until the mission has been completed or we risk putting her in danger without being able to kill the king.

Bauer guides us off course, looping around toward the outside of the forest. Releasing Gretel's hand, I wrap an arm around her waist to help support her as we slow to a quick walk.

"I'm fine," she puffs in response. She's anything but fine.

"We need to get out of the forest," Bauer informs us,

looking back. "We've lost the guards thanks to Gretel, but now they know we were there and will be searching the woods for you both—for all of us. We have to get you around people."

"You want us to blend in?" I ask.

Bauer nods. "You need to belong to whatever town you find yourselves in. We'll move quickly to get you to the palace district, but it's going to involve a little waiting while I clear the area before I bring you out in the open."

I study him as we move. I can tell he's nervous. His gait is stiff, though, I suppose that could be from discomfort since he isn't walking with his fake limp at the moment. Slowing again, he pauses until we catch up and slips his arm behind Gretel, under her arm, to help support her with me. The more we can do for her now, the easier it will be later.

"Hansel is going to kill me for this," Bauer grumbles.

"Probably," Gretel offers meekly. I blow air out of my nose instead of laughing to let her know I got that she was joking, but I'm too tired and too focused on our movements to offer a real laugh.

"Not much farther, girls," Bauer adds softly. "Once we reach the tree line, I'll get you two hidden, and I'll make sure the guards have already swept the area. Then I'll come back for you two."

"Okay," I agree quietly. I've done far too much running the last two days, especially for a baker who focuses on building muscle through lifting heavy bags of cooking ingredients.

"It looks like that's the town up ahead." Bauer nods forward.

If I strain, I think I can hear music coming from the streets of whichever town we've stumbled upon—possibly Gimpenlaug or Perihausen. If the music is so loud, that has to be a clear sign that the guards haven't left yet.

"There," Bauer says, pointing. "There's a large cluster of trees growing together. You can rest there and use the tree to hide yourselves if need be."

If we must, I'm sure Gretel could cause the five trees to swirl together, locking us inside until help can come, safe from whatever guards we might run into. We'll have given ourselves away, but at least Gretel will be protected until then.

I guide my charge to the trees, helping her to sit in the makeshift seat the trunks have formed. Glancing around, I make sure no one else is near, even though Bauer swept the area before he disappeared through the trees.

"Are you all right, Gretel?"

"I'll be fine," she murmurs. "This running thing is for the *guards* though. No one else should be subjected to this nonsense."

"Your brother trained you." I give her an incredulous look, "There's no way he didn't teach you how to run."

"Oh, I can run, Annika," she grumbles. "I just don't like it."

"Well, I can't say I blame you there. How long are you going to need?" I pray she doesn't need more than a few days to recover from using herself up over this.

"I'll be ready," she answers.

I sidestep as a cricket leaps past me, frightening me enough that I gasp—I forgot they like to act like rockets being shot at neighboring countries this time of year. It pings against a branch as it lands.

"I hate those things," Gretel voices my own thoughts. "I'll be ready, though, Annika. You don't have to worry."

She sounds stronger and less winded, but I know it's an act—like one of my illusions. It's a pretty façade to put people at ease. I've even done it to keep others calm around me. Poor Hansel has been a victim to my charms a time or two.

"We're going to be okay," she says, taking my hand. "You'll get me where I need to go, I'll do what I need to do, and we'll handle the rest of it. It will all work out, you'll see."

She's wise not to give any details of our plan while out in the open, but she's Hansel's sister so I should expect nothing less.

"Any chance you still have some of that peanut butter fudge in your pocket that you slipped my brother earlier?"

"Sorry, dear. We can make more later if you'd like." It wouldn't be terribly hard to make more of Hansel and Gretel's favorite candy. I know the recipe by heart these days.

"At least Hansel will know how to find us," Gretel changes the subject. "Good thinking on using the fireflies."

"We might have to use yours soon, too, if we go any further."

Gretel reaches to tap on the pouch on her hip just as the explosion goes off. I drop to the ground, pulling Gretel down with me. Overhead, a firework crackles in the bright blue sky.

"What in the name of lollipops is going on here?" Gretel's face scrunches up as we try to see through the trees.

"I don't know," I respond.

It's hard to see the colors in the light of day, but the remnants of the white glow slowly falls down from the sky. A second screaming collision with the air frightens us again. I lurch back against the tree, trying not to be too obvious about jumping.

"If the lanterns meant something—even if it *was* Bauer —do you think these fireworks mean something?"

"We have to assume that it does, but this time, Bauer hasn't had enough time to reach the fireworks at the center of the town. Something else is going on here."

I listen for the sounds of music coming from the town, but it's strangely silent. A third firework goes up in the air. Peeking around the tree, I look for signs of life along the edge of the town, hoping someone might be walking by and I could gauge their reaction to the fireworks. No one is there.

Another minute passes before I hear it—the sound of screams.

"It must be the guards," I whisper. "They've probably caught someone."

"What should we do?" Gretel struggles to turn around so she can see toward the town as well. I wrap an arm around her waist as she leans to the other side of the tree.

"Stay hidden, Gretel." I pull her to my side and she sighs.

The wind kicks up, knocking leaves off of the trees. They cascade around us like yellow raindrops. The rustling covers up the sound of crunching leaves for a moment—just long enough for us to lose our edge.

We turn at the same time, hearing the boots stomping through the woods. Gretel's face pales. She reaches out, getting ready to hide us if need be. I grab her hand, pinching it tightly—she can't do anything else to conceal us, or the assassination attempt is over before we've been able to do anything, and since *I* don't have time to make a *real* cake now, the king will probably have me executed.

Still holding her hand between my fingers, I flick my

other wrist, causing a shower of illusion leaves to fall between the men and us—they likely won't notice fallen leaves disappearing as much as they'd notice tall trees suddenly poofing out of existence when I get too far away, so I don't create any illusion trees for the moment.

As the shower of greenery continues, I pull Gretel toward the town. We're going to have to face the guards in the town if we want to escape the ones we're leaving behind, whose sole attention would be on the two of us in the woods—I'll take a distracted guard over a group going after two lone women in the woods any day.

We stumble the first few feet, but the buildings are close enough that we dart behind the first one while the leaves are still coming down in front of the king's men. Glancing around, I assess the situation. Gretel clamps down on my hand, as she's been trained to do so we don't lose her in a situation like this. Our jobs have always been to protect her; Gretel's job is to make sure she doesn't get separated from us.

The buildings have a pink tone here, and while there are a variety of bright colors—pink seems to be the over-whelming hue of this street. Even the glass in some of the shops is tinted with rose. Doors slam shut all around us, though they aren't closing because of us—they're afraid.

I have to find somewhere to hide Gretel. Not knowing who we can trust, I put an illusion over us, changing our appearance so no one could find us.

"That was bold," Gretel chirps at me.

"We don't have time for subtleties right now," I growl back. I didn't mean to sound so harsh, but I left all my sugar back at the bakery. "There."

I haul the girl across the street, nearly colliding with a man and his son as they maneuver away. He curses but doesn't stop.

The old woman who waved me across the street can barely hold up the cellar door for us, but she waits until we're safely inside before letting it slam shut. I climb down the stairs, refusing to relinquish Gretel's hand.

Once on the dirt floor, the old woman points to where she wants us to go. I can't question it; we're underground, and the old woman only wants to be safe too—she doesn't mean to harm us.

She nods to the wall as she runs her hand over it. It clicks, revealing a hidden door. Just as she pulls it open, a firefly slips from Gretel's pouch, blinking in the dark cellar. The woman's head snaps over to the bright light.

My hand lashes out, concealing the device.

"I got it," I whisper as if I'd killed the bug. Holding my hand closed tightly, I try to block the light and conceal it behind my back. When the woman turns away, I slip it into Gretel's pouch. She tightens it so the rest can't escape to do their jobs.

The room smells like damp earth, but the woman

touches a switch and a dim blue light fills the room, just enough to give us limited visibility.

"What did you see?" the woman asks. When hiding from the guards of Candestrachen, information is coveted and often the only means of survival.

"Nothing," I inform her. "We weren't here when it happened. Do you know what the fireworks were about?"

"You weren't here, and yet you're here, girlie. Where were you?" She doesn't answer my question.

"We were in the woods, collecting firewood. What were the fireworks about?"

"The guards found some rebels, I think." She waves her hand, referring to the resistance—she must not be one of us. "Whether they are or not, I'm sure we'll have an execution. Levin will be thrilled."

It's strange to hear her refer to the king without his title, but I like how it removes some of his power. I might have to try that sometime.

She eyes my new, curly red hair.

"Are you two sisters? Surely you aren't mother and daughter."

"Sisters," I inform her, picking up Gretel's hand. "We live with our mother over—"

My words are cut off as the heavy sound of a body trying to break through a door fills the space we just left. The guard pounds again on the outside cellar door.

"There's another way," the woman whispers. She

hobbles across the blue-lit room. Opening another door, she motions us through. Maybe she is resistance. From the corner of my eye, I see her shutting the door behind us. "Go to your mother."

I try to protest, but she stays behind, shuffling back across the room to save us. Knowing we can't stop, we press forward, groping the walls to figure out where we're going in the dark.

"Ow." I gasp as I run into the bottom step of a staircase leading upward. Gretel bends down to feel what's ahead of me.

Carefully, we climb to the top, looking for a latch that will let us escape. "The firefly," I remind her. She pulls one of the tiny devices out of her bag and holds it between her hand. Every time it blinks, we search for the way out.

Finally, the door clicks. Gretel puts the firefly away, brushing back her now-brunette hair—a new illusion I cast meant to keep people from asking too many questions. This time, I look old enough to be her mother, and Gretel looks at least a few years younger than her age.

She nods, and I crack the door open to see what's outside. The street is quiet, so we hurry outside, closing the door behind it—it blends in perfectly with the side of a stone wall.

"Let one of them go," I instruct. "He's never going to be able to find us at this rate."

Gretel follows my command to leave a trail for her brother as I notice a pile of stacked logs at the end of the street, nearly on the corner. If we can hide behind it, we'll be able to see through the logs but won't be likely to be seen. I'll have to watch for snakes hiding in the firewood, but they're our least dangerous enemy at the moment.

This street is filled with colorful pastel houses, each boasting awnings and shutters of different colors. As we reach the end of the street, I try to determine if we're about to enter a pit of vipers more deadly than the king's guards, and then we duck behind the wood.

Through the holes in the cut fire logs, I can see out onto the street. It seems strange now that the fireworks have stopped—though they stopped before we ran into the cellar—and the sound of footsteps is overwhelmingly loud next to us in the explosions' absence.

The guards pass by, oblivious to two strange girls on the ground mere feet from them. The logs protect us from view, giving us the advantage. I eye the top of the stack, trying to decide if any of the pieces could make a good weapon.

When the street is quiet for a moment, I add a few illusions to the stack of wood, making faux pieces stick out farther than the rest to keep passersby at a distance. Gretel fidgets nervously beside me, and I wonder if that's what she does when I force her into barrels and that wooden cake meant to take down the king of Candestrachen.

The noise flairs up again down the street. With the logs sticking out perpendicular to the street, I can't see anywhere but straight ahead, leaving me to guess what is coming. Someone is struggling against the guards, but the shouts of the men overpower the person being dragged down the street.

A young boy is pulled past us, kicking and screaming. He lifts his feet off the ground, hoping to drag the men down with the sudden shift of weight, but he's small and doesn't carry the weight he thinks he does. Gretel tugs at my sleeve, but there's nothing we can do.

The boy's hat falls off and is quickly trampled by another guard. The man shoves the boy as he dangles in the air between the other men. The child kicks his legs as if he's running, trying desperately to find any kind of traction with which to turn himself around to confront the older man.

Gretel buries her face against my arm, not wanting to see the boy in the light blue shirt and suspenders dangling in the air. He looks to be around her age, and I know this is the image she will carry with her as we wheel her into the palace in a few days.

The boy shouts as the older men yell over him, taking him further down the street. Just before my line of sight is cut off, I see the far guard angle himself—they're turning. Throwing my hand out to the side, I nearly collide with Gretel as I force an illusion of darkness between us and the street we just vacated. The guards pass by without seeing us.

A few agonizing minutes later, we hear the wails of townspeople, pleading with the guards. I hold my breath, knowing the sound that's about to fill the air. A tear slips out of my eye as the poor boy dies from the small charge they tied around him somewhere a few streets over.

"We need to go, Annika," Gretel says, tugging on my arm. Her voice has a hard edge to it. "We need to go home."

Before she can do anything else, more footsteps approach. Gretel leans back against the side of the building, not wanting to see this time. A few women's dresses swish by us in a rainbow of colors. They hurry ahead, not wanting to slow in front of the guard coming our way.

Their ankles twist as they look back to see the men approaching, but they don't lose their step. Their words mesh together as they speak, but I hear something about a rebel leader.

"Make way," a guard calls. His voice is deeper than my father's was. It's startling to hear. I've always associated my father with the deep tone of his voice and the scent of cinnamon, and the sensory connection is so strong, I can nearly smell the spice in the air.

More people walk by, and I realize they aren't trying

to escape at this point—they're following orders. This is a parade.

They've caught someone.

Legs position themselves in front of the openings I was looking through, so I scoot down, trying to get a better line of sight. Gretel follows, curiosity getting the better of her.

It's easier to see around men—they have wide stances, but the women's dresses make it impossible to view anything. Judging by the number of people I can't see around, I'm guessing there's at least fifty people out there —it's enough for us to blend in. The guards have someone in their grasp, so they shouldn't have time to bother with the likes of what appears to be a mother and daughter mixed into the crowd.

"Blend in," I hiss, poking Gretel until she moves.

Once in line, we hover behind a man and woman, trying not to look as nervous as the young girl standing next to them. Guards pass by, weapons ready as they glance over the crowd, eyes glazed now that their job is done and they've chosen a victim.

"Get back, you swine," the deep voice calls again. I search the crowd for him, bobbing around heads as they move in and out of my line of sight.

Someone is kicked. Air rushes from the man's lungs as he crumples back into the crowd a few yards down. A log flips as he grabs hold to steady himself, sending it flinging into the street nearly colliding with a guard. The king's man pauses, glaring at the man who stumbled. One of the other guards whispers something into his ear, and the angry man looks away, letting the townsmen live another day.

The group sways, forcing their victim forward. I can't see around the tall guard standing in the front, his uniform blindingly bright.

Gretel wraps her arm around my hip in case we need to run. I wish I could brush back her blonde hair, but my illusion has covered any trace of the girl we raised to be an assassin. Gretel has always looked like an innocent child, but the dark hair similar to mine makes her look even more angelic.

The mass of guards steps closer, yelling about what happens to rebels and traitors when they're caught by the king's men. The speech is different than the usual one—though perhaps that's because we're in a different town and the guards take a different tone here.

"This man is accused of leading the rebellion against His Royal Highness, King Levin and his armies. You know what happens to traitors and liars, but this man is worse than any treacherous scum slithering through our streets of Perihausen! He is the leader of all of the rebels and charges have been brought against him by one of his co-conspirators for plotting to destroy the king and his kingdom!

"He is being taken to the palace where he will be brought before the council and justice will be leveled upon him. King Levin will decide how to handle this kind of atrocious behavior and this man will pay for his crimes, as will the sniveling rat that pointed him out to us."

The guards sneer around him in response.

I'm sure the man who accused the leader was only trying to survive, but it backfired on him, and now two men will die instead of one—both a bigger spectacle than the guards had thought.

The tall guard moves, swaying to reveal the rebel leader behind him. Gretel nearly falls next to me, clutching at me to hold herself up.

Bauer.

CHAPTER 5

Our leader fixes his eyes straight ahead, refusing to look to the left or the right. He's adopted his limp again, heavily leaning on one of the guards each time he steps with that foot. His shoulders are back, and his head is held high as the guards parade him through the streets.

Unlike the young boy earlier, Bauer will not die today. He will be put on trial and accused of whatever the younger man blamed on him to escape death and anything else the king hurls at him to put on a good show.

His death will be far more complicated than an explosive wrapped around his mid-section in the center of town, standing on a platform for all to see the spectacle. No, Bauer's death will be a celebration unlike anything we've seen in Candestrachen.

A firefly takes off through the crowd, rising above the heads of the men and women forced to cheer the death of someone they'd rather help save—no one knows who Bauer is, but if the king wants him dead, they assume he must have done at least something to help the people of Perihauser in their minds.

I turn to Gretel to see if the firefly is hers as it flies through the crowd. A deft nod is my answer, her eyes fixed in horror on Bauer as they lead him past us. The mechanical firefly blinks in front of Bauer, almost as if it knows him. The man flinches for the first time, and I can tell by the tiny tick in his neck that he almost turns to search for us. He forces himself to stay still, refusing to accidentally give us up.

If Gretel weren't with me, or if I didn't need to finish the cake and take it to the palace to complete our mission, I'd risk myself and create an illusion to distract the guards, kicking them or pushing them long enough for Bauer to have a chance at escaping. I'm not alone though, and I know what Bauer would command me to do—protect the mission at any cost.

The guards harass him and the other man as they walk by. People scream insults at the two traitors, knowing what is expected of them. They try to hide the defeat and sadness in their voices so they aren't called out as sympathizers.

As soon as they round the corner, people turn back, peeling away from the group. Much like they do in Leipden, they run into homes and businesses, trying to stay out of sight. I move with the flow of the group, pulling Gretel along behind me. She matches my pace, never stumbling—I wonder if she's regaining her strength or if it's fear pushing her forward for the moment. It's often in moments of great weakness that we find our deepest wells of strength and do the impossible, at least, according to my father.

When we reach the end of the street, I slip into the shadows. It's still day, and while the shadows aren't dark enough to hide us, they offer us at least a little concealment, and we move. It's cooler in the shadows of the buildings than it is in the sun and I suddenly realize just how strong the wind is.

Leaves gather around our feet as I slow us, trying not to draw attention by running now that we're away from the crowd. Each step elicits crunching noises, and I worry we might be overheard.

The edge of the town is quiet, but people still loiter around as if the guards hadn't just been there. The men aren't using their brains, but if they want their heads on a spike, that's up to them.

Before stepping out, I cause a fountain to appear on the far side of them. Water bubbles up from the ground, slowly at first—enough to go unnoticed—but once it's a few inches high, it starts to get attention. The men turn, trying to figure out where the water came from.

With their backs turned, I point Gretel to the woods. I entice the illusion water higher—knee level, then up to their waists. As they reach out, I cut it off, pausing for a moment before it springs up again. Gretel guides us to the safety of the woods while I distract the men who could possibly turn us in later on if they think it might save them when the guards inevitably find them out here. When we're far enough away that I'm straining to see, I cut it off, leaving the men confused.

"I know," I cut Gretel off. "We'll figure out how to get Bauer back."

"No, we won't, Annika. The mission is in one week. If you think the king won't kill Bauer as part of the celebration, you're crazy." She sounds like her brother—practical, logical, mission first.

"We can complete the mission *and* save him."

"*No*, Annika, we *can't*. We both know it." Gretel's arms shake once as if her entire body wants to convulse but can't because she's holding her muscles so tight. She swallows, breathing heavily. "Think this through—what is he going to do?"

She's not talking about Bauer; she means the king.

"He will move up the event because you're right, he *will* want it as part of the celebration, but he also doesn't let his enemies live long. He will move the ball up to match the execution."

"Which means we have to go back," she whispers. "We have to follow the markers, Annika. We can't stay."

I close my eyes, taking a deep breath. I'm supposed to be the logical one here, and yet, I'm being emotional. Of everyone who was willing to die for this mission, I didn't expect Bauer to be the one to actually make the sacrifice—he wasn't even supposed to be in the palace. Frankly, I assumed it would be me—Hansel and his sister are far too resilient to die at the hands of King Levin and his whims.

"There," I point, catching sight of a glowing blue dot in the distance.

We make our way through the trees, walking at a normal pace. There's no need to exhaust ourselves yet. We've got a few hours before darkness falls and if we arrive late, the guards will likely have left my little bakery home, giving us time to make preparations for the new date the king is bound to shift to.

If my calculations are correct, we'll have no more than three days until his tolerance gives out and he wants to end Bauer. Our leader, on the other hand, will hold out until his dying breath. He will never give us up, but he'll hold out long enough to give us time to get everything into place so when we come to his funeral-masquerading-as-a-ball, we'll be ready to kill his executioner to prevent it from ever happening again.

The walk is long, much longer than the run. The wind gusts around our clothes and I realize I can drop the illusion I've been holding around us since we were in the town. My pink dress moves around my ankles, picking up stray leaves and pieces of debris.

We walk in silence—there's nothing to say. Bauer will die. We'll have to work night and day on the cake to be ready. Hansel will find us eventually. The king will die—there's nothing we can change until he does.

Another blue firefly blinks ahead, hovering in a bush. I open my hand, picking it up and returning it to the pouch on my hip. By the time we find the next two, the weight of the day has crashed over me, and I feel exhausted.

"Are you feeling any better?" I ask softly.

"I'll be fine," she replies. "Even if it moves up, I'll be fine."

She will have to be.

I didn't realize how far we'd traveled until it took half an hour to locate the next firefly. We nearly took the wrong path, but Gretel saw it blink in the distance on the opposite side of the fork. I have to squint to see it as she points.

Another twenty minutes and we find the next firefly, its blue glow bouncing off a tree as the sun shifts in the sky. The clouds take on a pink light, tinging everything a strange shade of red-gold.

"Annika!" Hansel's voice startled me. I jump, spinning to face him. I hadn't heard him approach, though, no one ever does if he doesn't want them to.

"Hansel."

"Hansel!" Gretel charges past me toward her brother.

Aurik stands next to him, Brahms just behind. All three hold axes in their hands—innocuous enough to be played off as if they were leaving work, but deadly enough to take down anyone who got between them and Gretel.

Hansel steps forward, dropping his weapon to the side. Gretel throws herself against her brother, and he wraps his free arm around her.

"What happened?" he demands.

"Bauer showed up," I inform them. "The guards were on their way, and he came to get us out."

"There were guards in the woods," Gretel continues. "They came for us."

"We made it to Perihausen. A woman hid us, but it didn't last long. We hid in the crowd and discovered that someone had turned Bauer in as a rebel leader. They have him, Hansel."

His face pales. Tension lines form around his eyes as he drops his arm from his sister's waist.

"They'll move up the ball," I say.

Hansel nods. "We need to get back. The bakery is fine —no one was there when we arrived. It looked like they did some damage to your cover story supply though."

"The cake?" I inquire. I'm terrified if they found the extra food, they might have also found our delivery method.

"You did a good job hiding it." He nods to Gretel.

"What did you do?" I turn to the girl. She hadn't had enough time to hide it when Bauer came in.

"I slipped a few of your plants in." She tries to shrug casually.

"She covered it with greenery like it was a massive plant stand." Hansel chuckles.

"She even added some trays of bread to it as if they were cooling there," Brahms adds.

"It was pretty inventive." Aurik cocks an eyebrow, shooting Gretel an impressed look.

A worried look fills Hansel's face when I glance at Gretel. She stares back at me defiantly.

"What did you do?" Hansel's voice comes out as a whisper.

When Gretel doesn't speak, I answer for her. "There

were guards in the woods—apparently there are *always* guards in the woods now—and Gretel moved the trees again."

"But we didn't see anything shift." Aurik's statement comes out like a question.

"Further down," I inform him. "It wasn't the entire forest this time."

"Hansel, you've been holding out on us about your sister," Aurik protests good-naturedly. "We could have borrowed her last year for that big project—"

"No, we couldn't have." Hansel silences him. "She has a bigger purpose, and we're dangerously close to having that opportunity destroyed."

They grimace at his protective tone. Stepping away from the other men, Hansel pulls Gretel aside, whispering harshly. "How bad?"

She murmurs but I can't hear her reply. Aurik and Brahms glance at me uncomfortably—none of us like being caught in a sibling argument but there's nowhere we can go.

"We can't risk it," Hansel argues, still whispering loudly as if we can't hear him. Gretel quarrels back, crossing her arms over her chest. After a moment, she flings her hands out to the side, catching herself just before she shouts.

"Okay, that's enough," I interrupt. "We need to get back to the bakery. We have to replenish whatever the guards ruined and finish the cake because we all know Levin is going to move this stupid ball up and we'll all be in trouble if we're not ready on time."

The three men look taken aback when I use the king's name without his title. I like their reaction to it.

"She's not ready—" Hansel protests.

"I'm fine!" Gretel shouts, disturbing two birds sitting in different trees. They flap their wings at the same time, taking off in a similar direction.

"It doesn't matter," Brahms interjects. "Annika is right. We have to get back; we can handle this discussion there, no matter what we choose."

Hansel broods as his friends start to walk away, guiding us back to the bakery. I take Gretel by the arm, spinning her to follow them. After a moment, I hear Hansel's footsteps crunching behind us in the fallen leaves.

He stalks behind us for a few minutes, but eventually lengthens his stride and takes his place by Gretel's side. Hansel glances over Gretel's head to make eye contact with me. He clearly isn't happy, his narrowed eyes are a clear indication of that, but he softens his gaze, silently asking for my opinion on his sister's condition.

I think about it for a moment. If Gretel is sure she can handle the mission, we have to trust her. I understand why Hansel is so worried—I'm worried too—but this has to be Gretel's choice. She knows herself better than we do.

Gretel barely comes up to my shoulder, so I'm pretty familiar with the top of her head. Her hair parts in the middle, cascading down into long white-blonde strands on either side in a shiny curtain that protects her from the world when she hides behind it like I used to as a child. Somehow, looking down on her at this angle makes her seem even younger.

I nod.

Hansel purses his lips and nods back, closing his eyes for only a moment—he trusts us to make this decision, even though he doesn't like it.

The rest of the walk back to the bakery is quiet, comprised of stiff steps and dark moods.

The outside of the bakery is just as I left it earlier today, though it glows in the setting sun. I anticipate the fireworks display will be brighter and longer tonight in celebration of Bauer's capture. Brahms informed us that the fireworks earlier were also to announce a capture, this one in Gimpenlaug, though we haven't discovered who the king's men caught yet.

We trudge up the steps, and I want nothing more than

to lean against Hansel's arm and let him drag me up the stairs to the bakery. He's too busy keeping Gretel upright.

The moment we get inside and close the door behind us, Hansel takes her upstairs to rest. Brahms and Aurik look to me for instructions.

"We're not going anywhere, so you might as well put us to work," Brahms says.

"He meant *you might as well feed us*," Aurik corrects.

"You can have whatever the guards didn't take." I make my way to the back where I had set everything out of sight.

The room is practically empty. While they didn't tip anything over or destroy it, the guards helped themselves to the sweets and treats laying around the bakery. I'm sure if the king's cake had been baked and ready to go—assuming it was a real cake—they probably would have devoured that without a second thought as well, leaving me to take the fall if I didn't recreate it in time for the ball.

"Looks like there's some bread and cookies over there, boys, help yourselves." I wave at the remnants of the trays. It's a shame Bauer hadn't delivered that massive fake flour order I had placed yesterday...I have a feeling I'm going to need it to replace everything.

"Where do we start, Annika?" Brahms asks softly, touching my arm like Hansel might have before we became close.

I sigh. At least they're willing to help.

Pointing things out, I set them to work collecting materials for me while I walk into the other room to start the ovens. I don't bother playing with the fire, knowing Hansel will be down momentarily to start it.

As if on cue, the fireplace lights up, casting the room in a deep orange tint. Sidling up behind me, Hansel wraps his arms around me.

"Hansel, what if they see?" I shrug him off, attempting to slip away. He catches me by the hip and spins me, pinning me against the oven.

"Those two?" He grins, cocking an eyebrow at me. Hansel leans toward me. "What do you care? Let them find out."

"Find out you two have been making out for weeks?" Aurik walks into the room, arms full with bags of flour and sugar.

"Oh, whatever will we do when we find out *that* news?" Brahms asks innocently.

"Why, we might just die of shock." Aurik continues, setting down the supplies on the large table.

"Wow, really?" Hansel retorts. He wraps his arms around my waist. "Fine, if there are no secrets here…"

His lips touch mine softly, which is shocking considering the force with which he moved toward me. My hands rest on the crooks of his arms, and I let him kiss me publicly for the first time. The men ignore us for a moment before telling us to knock it off.

Hansel brushes back a strand of my long hair.

"I like not having to hide," he whispers just loud enough for me to hear. "And apparently, we were terrible at keeping it a secret anyway."

"*You* were. *You* were terrible at it. *I* had no one to keep it from."

Since I lost my father, all I've had was Hansel and his sister. Bauer too, I suppose. If anyone gave our secret away, it was Hansel.

"I think Gretel knows, too," he murmurs as he kisses me again.

"Oh, she knows."

"We *all* know," Aurik snaps. "What we *don't* know is how to bake this stuff. A little help here, Annika?"

The two motion at the table littered with supplies. I pull away from Hansel and start to direct the baking efforts. Once I have Aurik and Brahms settled, Hansel wheels the cake form out for me to begin my work. He leaves me alone to complete my task and takes his place alongside his cohorts.

I open and shut the lid a dozen times to make sure it will work. It doesn't so much as creak. When I'm satisfied, I begin to circle the wooden cake, formulating a plan for decorating it.

From the corner of my eye, I can see the three men

watching me as I stalk around my project, but they don't say anything as I work. My hands reach for the fondant.

I smooth every bit of the fondant over the cake form, leaving only the top uncovered. It only picks up bits of light over the carvings I created on it earlier, the rest is so dark that it almost looks like I pulled night from the sky and whipped it into the fondant.

The fireworks explode outside as if the king knew what I was thinking. Pink fills the sky, radiant and bold, as it announces Bauer's capture. Reds sparkle after it, followed by screaming white blazes of light. The show would be magnificent if it weren't so murderous.

We make our way to the porch to watch it in case anything is different about it. Like every night, the fireworks glitter in the sky, reflections bouncing off of the pointed rooftops.

Minutes go by and the show proceeds as normal, the only variation is the colors and styles of fireworks the palace and towns shoot into the sky simultaneously. Hansel rests his hand on my shoulder as I lean against the porch railing. I can smell the scones inside and turn to go and check on them. Hansel's hand trails after me, but he doesn't take his eye off the skies above us.

I duck into the bakery and remove the tray of scones from the oven. Setting them on the table to cool, I glance around to see if anything else needs to be attended to.

"What is *that?*" Aurik's voice fills the room.

"It can't be," Brahms responds, panic in his voice.

"Annika!" I run to the door when I hear Hansel's harsh call.

In the sky, an orange fireball curves up into the air. I exit the bakery only a moment before it transitions from a streak of orange with a long tail into what looks to be a fire with a tail of blue and purple, almost like the wick of a candle. When the light hits it, it changes again, becoming a white glowing cloud trailing after a tiny spec of orange as it continues to arc up into the night sky.

"What is it?" I ask.

"It's a rocket, Annika." Hansel sounds breathless. It's terrifying.

As if totally disjointed, the rocket separates, leaving the thick trail of clouds behind, only a thin line of almost-blue clouds connecting the now-white glowing circle to the tail end of its streak.

"Where is it heading?" Aurik murmurs. I have a feeling he already knows.

Suddenly, it's as if the rocket explodes, a large cloud of pulsing blue frills out from it like a petticoat some of the towns ladies wear under their massive skirts. It swirls around the glowing streak as it changes its trajectory, beginning its descent.

Another moment goes by and none of us speak, fixated on the rocket sailing through the night sky. Behind it, fireworks continue to go off as normal in greens and yellows. The clouds from the rocket suddenly widen, becoming a solid wave rolling off the bright white light guiding it through the air. Something flickers behind it, leaving the secondary glowing object to pulse out strangely-shaped clouds in two different directions as it keeps up with the part of the rocket in the lead.

Pieces of the rocket break off, drifting quietly to the ground, glowing just as brightly as the main rocket. The entire glowing mass tips down, propelling itself quickly toward the ground before I realize what's happening.

"Hansel, is that—"

"Perihausen." He confirms my suspicions only moments before the rocket collides somewhere beyond the trees. Small ripples can be felt in the floorboards under my feet, but I likely wouldn't have noticed if I hadn't watched the rocket slam into the ground as it wreaked havoc on the city where Bauer was captured only hours ago. I hope the old woman who helped us is safe.

The vapor trail still glitters in the sky as smoke drifts up above the tree line to meet it. The fireworks finish their explosive show, the last of the finale sparkling away in the cool night breeze as we turn to go back inside.

"At least it wasn't here," Brahms says, breaking the silence.

"The king wouldn't hurt his precious cake." I didn't mean to lash out.

"He didn't touch Leipden, at least," Aurik adds.

"But he destroyed Perihausen," I protest.

"We don't know that for sure yet." Hansel tries to calm me. "We'll find out tomorrow."

"You know he did," I say under my breath as I return to my cake.

The dark colors inspire me, and I set to work decorating the device that will deliver death to King Levin.

CHAPTER 6

I t's late morning when I finally wake up, no longer perched against the chair I was leaning on while icing the wooden cake. My blanket is warm around me, demanding I stay in place longer.

The floor is cool when my feet touch it. Hansel must have carried me upstairs after I fell asleep, but there's too much work to be done to stay in bed any longer.

Opening the curtains, I find that the daylight is unaffected by the spoils of last night's attack. Opening the window, I can faintly smell smoke, and I'm sure once I reach the first floor and can see out another window that there will be a dark trail of black smoke from the charred ruins of whatever remains of Perihusen.

Candestrachen lost a fine town last night to the king's whims.

Downstairs, Gretel is awake and working over the stove. Bacon, eggs, and French toast scents fill the air. Aurik stares in Gretel's direction hungrily. Brahms looks up as I approach.

"You shouldn't have let me sleep so long."

"Thank your boyfriend," Aurik calls over his shoulder.

"*Boyfriend?*" Gretel snaps, turning to look at me. "Is that what we're finally calling it?"

The front door swings open, revealing Hansel. His frame fills the doorway, backlit beautifully by the sun. His blond hair takes on a golden sheen as the breeze moves a few strands. The girls in the town have been throwing themselves at him for years…if only they could see him now.

"You're up," he mentions, moving across the floor. He kicks the door closed behind him, cutting off the sunlight.

"What did you find out?" Brahms asks.

"The ball has been moved up."

"To when?" Brahms inquires.

"Tomorrow." Hansel sounds grim, his face showing the wear of the day, dragging down his features.

"Tomorrow?" I gasp.

"*Tomorrow?*" Gretel's terrified voice jerks us all into action. We leap toward her, ready to comfort her. I reach her first, wrapping her in my arms.

"You'll be okay, Gretel," Brahms promises her as Hansel reaches us.

"We'll take care of you," Aurik adds. "No one will hurt you."

"Will you be ready, Gretel?" Ever the big brother, Hansel sounds as if he's ready to carry her off to safety right now and call the entire mission off.

"Can you get me out of there, Hansel?" she asks.

"Always. I will always get you out of bad situations."

"Than I will do this," she announces, gathering her confidence around her like a barrier between her and the world. "Annika, can you finish the cake?"

It's as if Gretel has suddenly been possessed by the girl in the mill, ready to take down the king. I have no doubt that she can kill the king and escape.

"I can finish it, but you have to promise not to do anything today, Gretel. You need to be as recharged as possible when we put you in that cake tomorrow morning."

"This is nearly a week before we expected it to be," Hansel responds. "We need to make sure everything is in order and that we don't forget anything when the time comes. We're rushing, and that makes me nervous."

"I can work on a list while I'm sitting around since I'm

not allowed to help." Gretel side glances at me. She adds quickly, "It will give me something quiet to do so I don't have time for my brain to stress out about everything."

"I'll get you some paper." I move away to find a notebook and pen for her.

When I return, I find her in a chair near the wooden cake—we'll be able to chat about the list while I work. Hansel stands behind us, observing the dark cake for a moment.

"Did he ask for that?"

"No." I shrug. "He said he wanted a cake to celebrate Candestrachen. What better way than to bring in the elements of the cities?"

"I don't see how—"

"You will," I interrupt him. "Now, go. You have work to do."

Aurik slips out the front door to prepare the other men for the change of orders. I have one day to complete this cake—in the morning, we have to deliver it to His Royal Highness.

"What *is* your plan for that, Annika?" Gretel asks as her brother steps away.

"The king is so fond of his candy-shaped rooftops and glittering light displays. I'm going to bring them to life on the cake."

"And his fondness for *death* will be included on the inside?" She smirks like her brother does.

"Yes, my dear, his death will most certainly be on the inside of his precious cake."

I lift the icing bag and begin to swirl large strands of bright pink frosting around the base of the cake. Walking around it, I cover it evenly with smooth lines of sugared perfection. After a while, I set the pink down and pick up an icing bag with white icing. Tracing along the same path, I mimic my motions, adding a thin white line next to each pink stripe.

Gretel mutters in approval, glancing up from her list for a moment before looking back down. I catch her staring at the cake when she doesn't realize I'm looking. I'm sure she's worried about everything, but the moment I look up as if I might glance over, she goes right back to work—I hope I'm helping keep her mind off of tomorrow.

In just over twenty-four hours, she'll be springing from the cake, prepared to touch the king of Candestrachen's hand. She'll pull the life from him, taking on every bit of darkness and soul inside of him. It will flood her over, threatening to break her.

I've seen her do it before—take life. Each time, it darkens her eyes, leaving her looking cold and lifeless. Though I've only ever seen her do it to plants, I know the toll it takes on the young girl's mind and body.

Hansel will not only have to pull her to safety once the guards realize what's happening, but he will have to use his power over light and *light* to pull her back from the evil she will have to take on. He's the only one that has the ability to rescue her and share the burden.

Along the top tier of the cake, I drizzle an off-white liquid icing, allowing it to dribble down the sides of the top tier of the massive cake. The droplets fall down, some reaching the top of the next tier, others ending relatively high.

I hand a bowl of sprinkles to Gretel. "Here, I know you were looking forward to this."

She grins and tosses a few handfuls at the drying icing. Most of them stick in place. I walk around, adding the colorful sprinkles to the sides she can't reach from her chair.

"So much for not working." Hansel snickers at us. Without missing a beat, Gretel tosses a handful of sprinkles at her brother's face. He reels back in surprise.

I join the young girl, tossing the tiny candies at Hansel...I'll regret it when I have to clean it up later.

Aurik walks in just in time to see Brahms and Hansel team up against Gretel and me. With a flick of my wrist, I transform the entire room into the candy-world illusion I had cast a few days before. The room springs to life with candy chandeliers and chocolate fountains. Swirled candies cover the banisters, and the fire pops in delight as I string illusion hard candies up by their wrappers from one edge of the fireplace to the other.

Brahms looks shocked as he turns to explore this sudden new world, eyes wide with delight. Aurik picks his jaw up and grins, frowning only when he realizes illusions aren't edible.

"Cruel," he comments.

"Isn't *everything* we're doing these days?" I counter.

"As delightful as this is, I have news," Aurik redirects us. "Bauer is to be executed at the ball tomorrow."

We grow somber as he explains the new plans for the party.

"The guards will be coming for you tomorrow morning, Annika. They'll escort you and the cake to the palace to see that nothing happens with it. I lied and told them I was your brother and that I would deliver the news of the rush order to you so they wouldn't come here themselves."

"At least you didn't say you were her boyfriend," Brahms jokes, glancing at Hansel.

"I would have turned him over as the witch they've been searching for if he had," I say sweetly, batting my eyelashes.

"I knew I liked you," Hansel adds, throwing an arm around my shoulder.

"You like me for my peanut butter fudge and my pastries."

"We've established that," Hansel replies, "but I like you for other reasons, too, like your quick sarcasm."

"It's her lips," Aurik jumps in. "Don't deny it. You're in it for the kissing."

"And that's enough of that, thank you," Gretel says shrilly. "We need to get back to work."

Aurik quickly relays the rest of the information he and his team found out, and we all settle back in to complete our tasks—the boys baking up our alibi, Gretel ensuring we won't forget anything, and me sugarcoating King Levin's demise.

"Open by order of the king!"

I wheel around to face the door. My hand dances in the air, concealing the scones, cookies, breads, and pies Hansel, Aurik, and Brahms had created. The candy-world illusion drops immediately, taking the sparkling sprinkles with it. Another flick of my wrist conceals Gretel behind a false wall with Aurik and Brahms as her protectors. Hansel is at the door before I can drop my hand.

I nearly drop the icing bag as I try to look natural as the guards force their way in.

"Where is the baker?" one demands.

Hansel looks to me.

"I'm the baker," I answer softly.

"By order of King Levin, we are to deliver you to the

palace." The guard eyes me carefully, slowly dragging his gaze over my dark red dress.

"I assumed as much," I reply, motioning to the cake. "I need a few more hours to finish the decorations."

I lean toward the cake, ready to continue my work. The guards grumble.

"Surely you don't mean for me to leave with a half-finished cake. What will His Majesty say?"

The guards protest rudely, but Hansel silences them. "The lady says she's not done, and your job doesn't require you to escort us there until the ball tomorrow. If you want to go out and have fun this evening, go. You don't need to babysit us while we're icing a cake. Come back tomorrow to collect us."

"Fine, finish the cake. We can go in the morning."

"We'll bring the vehicle first thing."

Strange, they didn't seem to have brought a vehicle to transport us this afternoon. Perhaps they were anticipating finding me flustered without the cake ready and thought they'd be taking me to be punished instead of lauded for my magnificent sugar creation.

They stalk out of the bakery and down the steps. The snake that chases them is my own design, slithering after them as one of the men screams long enough to make Hansel snicker beside me. The snake hisses, lashing out, only to disappear as the men run off.

"Testy now, aren't we?"

"I didn't like them." I eye Hansel. "They were planning on hauling me to the palace to stand trial."

"Ah, you noticed that too, did you?"

I drop the illusion as we turn back from the doorway.

"It's safe," Hansel announces. "We need to get this finished and ready to go, though."

"Did I hear you invite yourself along on the cake delivery?" Aurik asks, stepping away from his place along the wall.

"Better than trying to *talk* myself in," Hansel retorts. "The two of you are on watch duty tonight. If those guards come back, we have to be ready to get Gretel into place before they make it up the stairs. You can take turns standing watch while the rest of us sleep."

"We should stay down here by the cake," I comment, pushing back my hair. I wind part of it around my finger in a loose curl.

"Agreed. But first, we need to actually finish it." Hansel takes my elbow and turns me back to the cake covered in candies, swirls, and sugar designs. He whispers into my ear. "After you, mistress baker."

"It's a good thing you all need me tomorrow, or I'd have to end myself right now after a sappy line like that." Gretel pretends to gag. "Now fetch me a snack. I'm hungry, and I'm not supposed to do anything for myself."

She plops herself back down on her chair and waves for her brother to bring her a pastry.

"This only lasts until tomorrow, little sister," he warns her playfully.

"We'll see," she retorts, waving her hand again. "I'm killing a king, after all."

"You're rescuing Candestrachen," I add, holding the icing bag that I just scooped up out to her waiting finger. "Killing the king is just the method that gets us there. Don't forget that."

Hansel looks surprised, lips slightly parted as he returns.

"Don't ever forget that," he says seriously to his little sister, turning to her. It's important we protect her from what she's about to do—taking a life, even to save thousands, is a devastating, life-altering situation to be in. I imagine the poor girl will have a hard time coping with it after.

"Got it." She licks the white icing off her finger, making a popping sound for emphasis.

"Now let me see that list while Annika finishes this monster up." He kneels down beside Gretel, eyeing me from under his long, dark lashes. I turn away, not needing the distraction.

"Are you ready?" Hansel asks as we lean against the railing. Brahms and Aurik sit inside, giving us a few minutes alone on the porch to decompress before we turn in for the night.

"The cake is ready," I answer. "I *think I* am. I'm nervous. What if I can't hold the illusion long enough?"

"You can," he promises, taking my hand. "You've held massive illusions for very long periods of time. All you have to do is keep the three of us from being recognized once we get inside. The rest is up to Gretel and me."

"I'm nervous about that too," I confess.

"You don't think I can get her out of there?" I can hear the frown in his voice. The fireworks display has long since ended, but I almost wish Hansel would add a little lighting out here for us to see by since the moon is hidden behind the clouds.

As if reading my mind, a string of lights snakes its way around the column next to me, adding a soft glow as Hansel turns me toward him. His touch is warm against the coolness of the breeze.

"You're the only one that *can* get her out, Hansel." I sigh. "I'm just…I'm worried that something will go wrong. Our entire plan had to be rearranged and pulled together in one day. There are so many ways it could fail."

"We're going to be fine, Annika." He lifts the necklace off my neck, twisting it in his fingers. "I've always been able to find you by this when you were wearing an illusion. It has always been the *key* to reuniting us."

A lone cricket chirps in the yard somewhere. I nearly glance toward it, but I know we're having an important conversation.

"I'll be able to find you tomorrow, no matter what. And because of you and your necklace, I'll be able to find Gretel because of her necklace too. No matter what happens, no matter how many illusions you pull, I'll be able to recognize you."

I raise my hand, touching the gold trinket on the end of my mother's golden chain. It's a key with a burst of sparkling light at the top—a perfect representation of the lights Candestrachen is so obsessed with. In the palace, they'll catch the light and sparkle—even across the room, anyone who is specifically looking will notice it.

"I'm changing the plan, Hansel."

"What?"

My wrist brushes against the skin on his cheekbone, lightly brushing over his face as I move strands of his hair back from his eyes. He leans into my touch.

"I know we had planned to make Gretel a brunette and younger, but there's a better way now—the guards have handed it to us."

"What do you mean, Annika?" He reaches up and takes my hand, turning his face to kiss my open palm. It burns through me as if I accidentally touched the wire rack in the oven while adding a tray of uncooked muffins.

"The guards want a witch…we'll give them a witch. It won't be a tiny girl betraying the king, it will be the haggard old woman they saw in the woods that day. We'll give them their greatest nightmare—the woman who destroyed the forest and cost men their lives. They'll search for her until the day they die, but they'll never find a little blonde girl living with her brother in Leipden."

His lips are on mine as he mumbles, "You're brilliant." His fingers scrunch through my hair as he focuses on our deep kiss. I don't bother to stop him, even though our friends are only feet away inside the house. After an intense moment, I pull away.

"We should go in."

"Should we?" He grins.

"We need to sleep, Hansel. Tomorrow, we go to the palace."

He lets me lead him inside, holding his hand behind me with my arm stretched out as he pauses long enough to let me know he wants to stay.

Scooping up an apple from the table, he hands it to me as Aurik heads outside to take the first watch. Hansel sinks along the wall, waiting for me to join him a few feet from the cake form. I nestle against him, leaning against his shoulder and chest as I take a bite of the apple.

"It's always amused me how someone who bakes all these sugary treats could prefer healthy food like apples."

"A different kind of sweet, my friend."

"Well, I prefer your kind of sweet." He kisses my lips again. "Maybe apples aren't so bad after all."

CHAPTER 7

"Annika, it's time." Gretel shakes me gently. "Help me into the cake, Annika."

The room is deathly quiet aside from the snap of the fire and Gretel's tiny voice. Hansel and Aurik lay sprawled out on the floor, sleeping in different corners. Brahms stands on the porch, a sliver of his arm and side visible through the window.

"Wake up Hansel, and we'll help you—"

"No."

I blink at her.

"I will not say goodbye to my brother. I won't do it. I'll see him after, and that is that. Now, help me in before they wake up. We need to be ready when the guards arrive."

"Did you even eat yet?" I rub my eyes.

"I'll eat inside. You can hand me some snacks before you close it and add the final layer of icing." She tugs at my hand. "Please, Annika, I need to do this before I lose my nerve."

"Okay, okay." I stumble to my feet. "Go get whatever snacks you want, and I'll create the ladder."

I poke at my eyes again, trying to see straight. Blinking, I force my curls back. Separating my feet, I find my balance and stare at the cake. Terror washes over me—this is it.

My hands move slowly as if I'm conducting musicians. They flow through the air gracefully, and I picture the strangest set of stairs that lead from the floor, around the side of the cake in a wide arc. Railings appear on either side of the steps, swirling around the edges of the king's cake. I douse the entire thing in what looks to be pink swirled frosting and rock candy lollipops.

Gretel smiles softly as she returns.

"Gretel," I say, taking her hand as she sets her treats on the chair next to me. "I know you wanted to look a little different for this, but we've come up with a new plan—one where they'll never have any hope of finding you."

She raises an eyebrow at me.

"Gretel, you're going to be a witch."

"What?" She raises an eyebrow, her voice flat.

"From the woods. You're going to be the witch that rearranged the forest. A haggard old thing. When they come looking, they'll never expect to find a child."

She cringes as I use the word *child*, but she nods in understanding.

"I'm already the witch that rearranged the forest."

"But now you'll look like her."

"It's a shame not everyone has gifts like we do. It would make all of this a lot easier."

"It's a glorious thing that we are unique in this, Gretel, or we'd never pull this off—they'd be watchful of everyone. Besides, can you imagine what King Levin would do if he had the ability to do more than create fancy clothes with his gift?"

"He would be so jealous if he knew you could create illusions." She giggles quietly. "If he knew about you, you'd be stuck by his side for the rest of your life, transforming his little parties into even-more-grand events."

"You're probably right. Good thing he'll never find out." I take a deep breath. "Are you ready?"

She nods. Her eyes dare me to try to say anything that remotely sounds like a goodbye.

"Once you're inside, I'll seal off the top." I escort her to the first step. She places her hand on the rung of the railing and lifts a foot daintily. "You'll know when it's time to come out.

"I'll leave you in this form until we reach the palace and then I'll give you the illusion of an old woman. The ride will be long and probably bumpy, even with the motored machine. Try not to crash into the sides of the cake. If you need more air, you know what to do."

She nods, taking the next step.

"Try to focus on your surroundings. I'll be in the vehicle with you, so listen for my voice."

"I doubt they'll let you speak." She takes another step, allowing her to look down at me. My heart hammers in my chest with every step she rises into the air.

"Than just know that I'm there. Focus on every sound you hear. You'll be able to hear Levin's voice when he gets close enough to cut the cake.

"Be careful of the knife in his hand when you come out of the cake form. You're going to surprise him, and he might lash out. You need to be quick about it."

Gretel nears the top of the cake form, dressed in dark-colored clothes. She looks like an avenging angel.

"Do what you need to do, then get out of the cake, Gretel. Run. Hansel will find you, and I'll block however I can."

"I know."

"I'll find you when it's over, Gretel," I promise.

"I know you will, Annika. You've always taken care of

Hansel and me." She takes the final three steps, tipped down into the cake form. My fingers move, adding a few steps that disappear as she takes her foot off of them until she's standing up to her chest inside the wooden contraption. "I'll see you after."

She taps the sparkly necklace on her chest, and I tap on mine. Hansel will be wearing something similar on his coat pocket as well. All three charms shiny and noticeable, but nothing that can tie us together.

I hand the food to her and Gretel closes the lid, settling into the cake. I turn to find Brahms staring in the window at us. His eyes are glassy. He tips his head toward Hansel, eyes squinting as if asking why we didn't wake him.

I clutch my necklace in my fingers and smile. Nodding, I assure him it's okay, this is what needed to happen. Brahms sighs and turns back to his post.

I double and triple check my work once the top of the cake is concealed. When Brahms and Aurik switch places, I drag Brahms over to check my work.

"It's fine, Annika. You did good work."

"I'm sure it's fine," Gretel calls from inside the cake, her voice muffled by layers of fondant and icing.

"Aurik and I are going to try to rescue Bauer," Brahms confides in me quietly. "Hansel and Gretel will be our priority, of course, but if they don't need us, we're going to try to prevent the execution. We're hoping it takes place after the cake."

"You don't think he will use the cake to celebrate?" I frown. "And *you're* not even supposed to *be* at the palace."

"I'm sure he will, but maybe you could make something flash on the cake to keep drawing his attention all afternoon so he can't take his mind off it and he'll do it early."

"We have no idea when he will use the cake, Brahms."

"It's our best shot. Maybe we can get Bauer out in the chaos."

"Okay, I'll try, but I can't do anything to compromise Gretel."

"I would never ask you to." He touches my elbow.

"Thank you for risking yourself to try to save Bauer. You and Aurik could be safe in all this, but I'm really glad you're going to try."

"You three shouldn't be the only ones taking a risk today." He pats my hand. "Now, wake up Hansel and let's get ready. The light is peeking up, and I imagine the guards will either show up incredibly early or incredibly late."

"Gretel," I say a bit louder so she can hear me. "It's time to wake your brother up."

I want to give her as much time to prepare for his reaction as possible. Walking over to Hansel, I kneel down and touch his arm. He blinks awake, smiling for only a moment as he sees me before he remembers what day it is. He sits up quickly.

"Are they here?" He tosses a blanket off of himself and jumps to his feet.

"No, not yet." I take his hand. "We need to eat before they arrive though."

His eyes sweep the room.

"Where is Gretel?"

"She's ready, Hansel." It takes a moment before he catches on. His muscles tighten as he stalks toward the cake.

"Hansel, don't you dare upset her," I snap at him, whispering so Gretel can't hear. "She didn't want some big goodbye scene to throw her off. Tell her good luck and come outside to yell at me."

Hansel stares me down for a moment, jaw clenched. Glancing at the cake, tears fill his eyes. "I'm not going to yell at you," he whispers.

He looks like he's being torn in two, like some machine the guards use to torture people is shredding him right down the middle. I wish I could protect him from this like he's protected me so many times before.

"You good in there, Gretel?" he calls, gaze fixed on the floor off to the side.

"I'm fine," she calls back, sounding stronger than Hansel looks at the moment.

"Okay, I'm going to get something to eat and then I'll be back to walk through everything with you."

"Okay," she calls in reply.

I step forward and take Hansel in my arms—I know how hard this is for him. He lets me hold him for a minute, transferring his worry into our embrace. If I can carry even a little of it for him, I will.

His breath is shaky when he pulls away, but to his credit, his body doesn't show any signs of shuddering. He takes both of my hands in his, holding them near his chest.

"It will be okay, Hansel. We'll get her out of there."

"I know." He pulls away from me, sauntering over to the table for food. He picks up a palmier and holds it in his hands. After a moment, he takes a bite, looking like he might be sick. For as terrified as I am, it's so much worse for him with his little sister putting her life at risk.

"They're here." Aurik slips into the bakery from the porch.

Hansel swallows the rest of the sugary treat.

"Did you eat?" He shoved one at me. I gratefully devour it, wiping my hands on a towel before running over to the cake.

"Ready, boys?" I ask as Aurik and Brahms shove themselves against the back wall. I put an illusion wall between us as Hansel helps me move the cake. "Time to go, Gretel. We'll be with you the whole way. Just watch for the pendants."

She stays quiet, knowing her mission has started.

The motor on the vehicle roars loudly as the guards pound up the steps. I open the door before they can knock, inviting them inside. Before we went to sleep, we put away all of the extra pastries so the guards wouldn't see them, leaving only a tray out for us to eat this morning. I motion to it, inviting the guards to partake.

Hansel instructs them on how to help move the cake. Together, the three men lower the cake down the stairs and wheel it toward the brightly colored vehicle. Leave it to the king of Candestrachen to go overboard on the decorations on a motor vehicle.

The taller guard lowers the back, pulling down a ramp. The entire vehicle lowers to the ground, leaving the ramp as a mere decoration. Had they tried, they could have easily just lifted the cart with the cake into the vehicle.

As the men assist him, I take a small magnetic device and push it against the underside of the wheel well. Hansel reprogramed his fireflies to work in unison, so as we make our way from the palace after the assassination, we'll be able to easily find our way back to territory we know, no matter what happens.

The guards instruct Hansel to push the cake inside, nearly touching the seats in the front. From the sides, the men pull down extra seats and demand I get in. I climb up next to Hansel, taking a seat opposite him, positioning ourselves between the guards who follow us in and the cake.

A third man drives, steering us away from the bakery. Once they're sure we're gone, Aurik and Brahms will race through the woods toward the palace, slipping onto paths the vehicle can't take. They won't beat us, but it won't be more than an extra half hour until they arrive—it will give us enough time to be turned away from the palace and use illusions to slip back in, that way, in the aftermath, the baker can't be blamed because she was back at her shop, making pastries.

The road is less bumpy than I thought, the vehicle stabilizing us each time we hit a dip in the road. The cake is barely jostled as we move. If I didn't hate things the king oversaw so much, I might actually be impressed with their ingenuity.

Hansel watches me in the bouncing light of the vehicle. The sun shifts and changes as we drive under trees and around corners, casting long shadows at strange angles. He locks eyes with me, stretching his foot out quietly to touch mine, calming his nerves as much as mine.

I wish I could see out of the back of the motorized transportation, but there are no windows on the back doors. It's probably for the best—the guards can't accidentally see our fireflies and grow suspicious—but I wish *I* could check on them.

The journey stretches out, simultaneously taking forever and no time at all. The guards comment crudely as I step out of the vehicle to allow them to assist Hansel. Making sure no one is looking, I pull the magnetic container off the car and toss it away.

The men maneuver the cake out of the vehicle and onto the ground. They instantly wheel it up onto a marble ramp, taking it into the palace.

"Thank you," a woman with folded hands and a high collar says from the platform. "You may go now."

I start to protest, but she holds a hand up. "You are dismissed, young ma'am."

I blink. I hadn't anticipated being turned away so quickly.

"You don't want to come in here," she adds quietly. "This is no place for a pretty young thing like you. You will leave immediately. You've been thanked for your service, now go."

Her words leave no room for argument, but I've heard they prefer men take the accolades and praise inside the palace—I suppose this wise woman is why. I appreciate her looking out for me, but I value her unexpected part in our assassination plot even more—she has no idea she's giving me an even better alibi for the murder. At least I didn't have to come up with a reason for them to keep me out.

The woman hands me a few coins, not nearly enough to cover the cost of the cake if it had been real. I pocket it and turn to go. With the guards inside guiding the cake, Hansel and I are left to walk all the way back to the bakery.

Once we're out of sight, we round the corner to the front of the palace where large groups of people wait to get inside. Dignitaries hover near the front, flanked by townspeople doing their duty to show up to the frivolities.

My fingers dance, dousing me in shades of green. I release my hair from its bun and let it fall down to my waist. Hansel's breath catches as I look up. He's suddenly clad in an illusion dusty blue suit, with a long jacket reminiscent of the one Bauer was wearing when he was captured. I change Hansel's hair to a shocking red-colored that will ensure he is noticed in the crowd. My own hair morphs into a light brown that's not quite light enough to be blonde, but not dark enough to be brunette.

"I'm amazed at how stunning you look, even in different forms."

"You'd rethink that if you saw my haggard look from the other day," I joke. "Now, go get yourself into the palace. Good luck."

"Are you sure? That might be your best look of them all." He kisses my cheek, grinning. "After you, madam."

I make my way into the crowd, looking for an opening. If I can find a family or group, I might be able to sneak in at the end of their party without the guards noticing an extra person. The townspeople huddle together, acting like they're having fun, but there is nervousness in the depths of their eyes, and they quickly look away when I accidentally make eye contact with them. I hope they all make it out when the chaos erupts.

A group of men and women hover at the far edge, and I make my way over as the line shifts, allowing people into the palace. Slowly, I inch toward them. One step at a time, I get closer.

Suddenly, they sidestep, walking into the palace through a second door the guards open—I missed my chance.

"Well, what do we have here?"

I look up into the eyes of a guard towering over me.

"I'm here for the ball," I reply, batting my eyelashes. One of the perks of an illusion is that I can fix up my lashes when I need to.

"Are you now?" he asks. "Are you on the list?"

"Do I need to be?" I ask breathlessly. I could gag.

"That depends," the guard steps toward me.

From the corner of my eye, I catch sight of Hansel's illusion-red hair. He tries not to look horrified, but I can't miss his wrinkled nose and tight brow.

I take the guard's hand holding the list and stretch on my toes to lean over his arm. Pointing at the list. "There I am. Though, I'm not sure I'll be able to stay for the entire ball. If you see me coming out of those doors a little early, well, don't you fret. I just needed a little fresh air."

My toes curl in my shoes as I realize just how bad I am at flirting. I bat my eyes again, hoping to distract him from my ridiculous words.

His hand drops from the list as he transfers it to the one with the pen. It finds its way to my backside. "I'll keep an eye out for you."

I spin away, rushing toward the open palace door as he laughs behind me. Without bothering to wait for Hansel, I scurry down the hall to find my place in the throne room where the cake will be waiting.

If the outside of the palace was impressive, the inside is *inspired*. For as stunning as my candy-world illusions are, the interior of King Levin's palace is more spectacular and encompasses everything I created without any reference to candy.

Large columns shoot up from the floor covered in hand-carved vines and flowers. The marble floor is tinged pink and laid with small rivers of sparkling gold that course throughout the entire room. Chandeliers grace the ceiling every few yards with one massively large one hanging in the center.

Floor-to-ceiling windows allow the sparkling light to bounce through the diamonds placed into the crystal glass. Along the tops of the walls, there is a runner of precious jewels in every color, acting as a border for the room.

The cake sits by the throne—a massive silver thing made of arrows and dark metal. The king hasn't arrived yet, but once his crowd fills the room, I'm sure he'll make a grand entrance—he'll probably fly in on the back of a golden swan if the rest of this room is any indication of the lengths he will go to in order to impress people.

"Are you okay?" Hansel whispers harshly as he slowly walks by.

"Fine," I mumble—we can't be seen together. "Go away."

He steers himself across the room, positioning himself a dozen people away from the cake in the second row of the crowd. Pedestals with roses under glass cases dot my side of the room, and I pick a place next to a dark red one. I can tap it with my elbow if I need something to anchor myself to as I focus on everything around me.

Using my sleeve to hide my movements, I wave my fingers at the cake, adding a few small sticks around the tiers. If I need to get the king's attention, this will be how I do it.

The room grows louder as more townspeople enter. The dignitaries and visitors from other lands take places near the throne and in the stands off to the side left for guests of the king. Music swells up, and a number of couples dance as if it's their job—I'm sure it is—to make outsiders believe this is something we revel in every week. At least the king enjoys himself at these parties.

Heat creeps up my neck into my cheeks as more people fill the room. They mumble about Bauer out in the courtyard, locked in a cage with a rope around his neck, waiting for his execution. The dignitaries discuss it so loudly from their places in the stands that I can hear them taking bets on how the king will murder my friend.

The room feels like it's moving around me, but it's only overwhelm messing with my perception. A few deep breaths and I calm myself. I hope Gretel is staying focused inside of the cake. I move my fingers, transforming her into the old hag that claimed the forest as her own.

As her dress grows dark, and wrinkles form on her skin, I add a small piece of candy into her hand to let her know it's done. She can't eat it, but it will make her smile and give her a reason to relax. I picture her tucking her now-gray and matted locks behind her ear as she arranged her witch's dress to accommodate the space around her. We were only separated for a few moments, but she must have been terrified to be on her own with no protection or backup.

An hour goes by as more people file into the throne room. The noise is louder. Each breath makes it hotter. I lock eyes with Hansel once and his lips part, but I look away.

The world stops as Levin, King of Candestrachen walks into the room.

CHAPTER 8

evin struts into the room, a gold crown rests on his dark brown hair. Like me, he's wearing a green outfit, complete with a cape. For a moment, I consider giving Gretel a cloak with a hood to add to the witch's character, but the crowd needs to see she's old and a hood would cover that.

The king takes long steps through the center of the room as the crowd parts, bowing as he passes. He holds one arm behind his back, shoulders straight and head held high as he surveys this tiny sample of the kingdom crammed into his spacious throne room.

Slowly, he takes the steps up to his seat. Spinning

quickly, he makes a few women nearby gasp in surprise as he faces the room. The man sits, resting his hands on the ends of the armrests of his silver chair. One side of his lips tick up in a sickening smile and the crowd cheers.

Music pours out from the instruments in the corner of the room, the people playing them intentionally precise about every note. The chandeliers sparkle and I wonder how much Hansel is itching to change the colors of the light in them to shock the king.

The king waves his hand, and the dancing begins. People whirl around the room as I try to hide behind the glass-encased rose. Eventually, a man offers me his hand, and I have no choice but to allow him to lead me to the floor.

As I swirl, I try to find Hansel. Instead, the eyes I find are far more sinister—King Levin. He watches me for a moment as I dance. I try not to take notice, but it's hard to rip my eyes away from his piercing gaze. Does he remember me from outside Bauer's shop? He can't in my altered state, but I feel as though he knows everything about our plan as if he can read my mind.

The man swirls me one last time and I hurry off the floor with the crowd and Levin looks away, locking eyes with another girl and grinning wildly—no wonder the woman with the clasped hands warned me off. I huddle next to the rose again, watching the cake closely, but no one seems to be bothering it.

The king eventually gives a speech, ranting about the rebels and how easy it was to catch Bauer. He still doesn't know our leader's name, so he assigns one that doesn't fit Bauer at all.

The list of crimes is long, but we knew it would be. Outside, fireworks go off, giving me an idea. If I need to distract the king, now is the time for it.

I brush my thumb and pointer finger together as if I were snapping, brushing the skin together enough that if I were in a silent room, I'd hear a quiet swish. The sticks I had placed in the cake earlier spring to life—sparklers— emphasizing the king's words just as he gets to the part about moving outside for the execution. He's picked a particularly painful way to kill Bauer, and if I can give him even the smallest chance of escape, I have to try.

Levin glances to his right toward the cake. If he wasn't so distracted by the sparking dessert, he might have spotted Hansel with his illusion-red hair glaring at him in the background.

For a moment, hope swells in my chest, and I actually believe we can do this—we can assassinate the mad king and take our country back. But then the king takes a step off of his platform toward the crowd.

"I'd like to thank you all for joining me today," King Levin addresses them, holding his hands out in front of him benevolently. "I know you weren't expecting to be here until next weekend, but with the rebels quelled here in the glorious kingdom of Candestrachen, I couldn't help but share my joy with you."

He takes another step, and several stewards rush forward to move the cake as Levin barely moves one finger toward it.

"Given this entire event has been rearranged, I think perhaps we should toss aside tradition on this momentous occasion and celebrate first—perhaps even *during* the execution of our enemy. Let him see us reveling in the life I've created for this kingdom—a life of happiness and generosity. Let him see what he tried to destroy and what he shall never have for himself. What do you say?"

The crowd cheers on command, raising hands into the air. A man starts a chant. The crowd picks it up, praising Levin and his wondrous works.

Men wheel the sparkling cake from its position off to the side to where it can be seen in front of the king, closer to the far side of the crowd as they wait for him to call it forward.

Any normal person would have noticed the sparklers should have gone out by now, but I hold them in place, sparking and glowing for the king as he monologues. He never even considers the sparklers wouldn't bend to his will.

Suddenly, the sparklers glow brighter, as if an entire cloud of light surrounded each of them—Hansel. I find him in the crowd, but his eyes are trained on the cake as they should be.

"Even our cake knows we've earned our treats today!" the king jokes as the sparklers glow, transitioning to a red glow. "I've never seen a cake so beautiful—just look at it! It's Candestrachen in cake form!"

He uses the words he sent to me when he requested the cake be made and I feel as if I've done my job well. It may be a fake cake, but the outside was crafted to perfection. Dark icing with pink and white swirls and streams of icing flowing down the sides mixed with sprinkles— the architecture of the kingdom ready to bite the king when he least expects it.

"Ladies and gentlemen," he continues. How can one man speak for so long? "Today we celebrate the quick thinking of our guards. We celebrate the takedown of a rebel leader who never stood a chance against the *greatness* that is Candestrachen. We celebrate a cake that represents the *greatness* of this nation, but first, we celebrate the death of a traitor."

He lifts the hand near my side of the room, and the doors fly open as guards stomp into the room. The cake keeps sparkling as everyone turns. Trapped between several of the king's men is the man who turned in Bauer.

They force him several steps into the room before kicking the backs of his knees, making him drop to the ground. A guard pulls a sword—a weapon I've never seen any of the king's men use before—and swings it at the man before any of us can react.

I've witnessed men and women being blown up by explosive devices before, I've even seen them being pulled apart in different directions, but I've never seen one die like this before—it's archaic and grotesque. Blood pools out, reminding me of the icing I dripped on the cake less than a day ago. People push back to avoid it touching their shoes.

"And now…cake!" the king proclaims. I turn back to find him grinning, looking every bit the madman we know him to be.

The group turns in horror toward him. Several women blanch, fighting to keep their hands by their sides instead of clutching their chests. Children fidgeted against their parents' legs, trying not to react.

I've heard stories about time slowing down when major moments occur in one's life—every sense becomes sharpened, every heartbeat is felt, everything is experienced in acute detail. That doesn't happen now, but I wish it would so I could be more aware of everything going on around me—it would let me protect the people I love easier.

The guards wheel the cake forward in front of the mad king, sparklers still spraying small sparks everywhere. Even if the king got close enough, the illusion wouldn't burn him.

The executioner walks up from the back of the room, drying off the sword on a piece of material he found somewhere. I wonder for a moment if the king planned it this way—he probably did.

Once the blade is clean, he hands it to King Levin with a slight bow. This wasn't a part of our plan—he could run Gretel through with that sword, and she has no idea the king is holding it. She likely doesn't even know how the man was killed across the room.

"Darkness once overtook us," Levin says, slipping back into his speech as he points at the black, fondant-covered cake. "But *I* have brought the light."

I twist my fingers together again just enough that the sparklers expand with his words as if on cue. I can see Levin's eyes widen in surprise, but he grins as if he knew it was coming.

"I've brought life back into this nation and have given it a reason to thrive. We live in a land of luxury that cannot be found in any of our neighboring kingdoms." He turns to his guests. "We welcome you here, my brothers. There is none greater than Candestrachen, and your friendship is welcome here."

He glances around to his guests, selecting which will be honored. He nods to an old man with a gray beard reaching halfway down his chest. The man returns his nod, lips tight.

Levin turns, his green jacket and cape moving gloriously behind him. A piece of his long, brown bangs flips in front of his eye, and for a moment, he almost looks like he could belong in the towns of Candestrachen, selling wares in a shop, attending parades, and courting young women. His sneer morphs his face into something dark and twisted, though, as his evil side creeps out.

The side of the top tier of the cake unlatches, moving just enough so I can see it. Gretel has clicked the button on the inside of the wooden cake form as she prepares to launch herself at her target.

I slice my hand through the air at my side, killing the sparklers on the cake as Gretel in the form of the most decayed old woman I've ever seen flies from the top of the cake. Her face droops, skin sagging off her shallow bones. Deep recesses under her eyes demand the light create shadows there. Her hands, while fast, show the wear of years, and her veins protrude deeply.

Tight sleeves wrap around her wrist, pointing down toward her fingers—a feature I'm sure the king would appreciate had he had time to see it. Black and gray lace swirl over the dark fabric of her dress. Her bodice matches the sleeves, flowing into a skirt she can easily pick up to run in.

Gretel's face shows no emotion as the king attempts to reel back in surprise. The sword catches on the bottom of the cake form. Instead of slicing through it like it would with a normal cake, it scrapes up it harshly, sticking before it reaches the middle layer. It tumbles from his hand, crashing to the floor, point still stuck in the wood of the cake form.

"The witch," he cries, his words loud above the quiet crowd.

Gretel reaches out, catching his hand in hers. She leans forward, squinting into his eyes. The more hers close, the wider his grow.

She mumbles something at him as he pales.

Everyone watches in horror as the king begins to fade. It happens so quickly that his guards don't know how to react. As if transforming into a male version of Gretel's witch form, the king begins to hollow, his face growing slim and skin sagging off his bones. His once-brown hair turns a vicious gray moving out from the roots to the tips.

It looks like he shrinks before our eyes, caving in on himself as Gretel pulls the life from him, leaving only the decay of death.

She doesn't move as she works, focusing solely on her victim. Hansel is fixated on the young girl in disguise, so I take up the responsibility of watching the crowd. No one moves...except the guard who brought the king the sword.

The king falls to his knees; Gretel leans forward with him, but the approaching guard moves faster than she expects.

"Look out!" someone in the crowd cries, warning Gretel.

A woman screams, distracting a few people. The guard isn't deterred though. I rush forward as our plan goes sideways.

The man in uniform pulls the king away, tossing him on the ground, half dead. Pulling the sword from the cake, he reaches for Gretel. I throw my hands out, creating a barrier around the girl. The wall snakes around people, forming an oddly-shaped room and a maze-of-a-hallway leading out of the throne room. People jump out of the way as the barrier races at them. I slip inside the wall before it races past me and I barrel toward Gretel.

She's in a daze, not moving. I try to pull her from the cake form, but she's trapped in a world of death and Hansel isn't here to pull her back from the horrors she's committed. With no other choice, I leap over the bottom tier of the cake form and push it down the corridor I've created.

Tears burn against my eyes as I realize we've failed and now the only way out is through this maze I've built us. Even if we escape it, where can we go? How can we escape the palace? If I extend the escape outside of the palace walls, they'll just follow it and catch us when I lower the illusion wall. We have no hope and no means of finding freedom.

"I'm so sorry, Gretel." My words come out mixed with tears.

At least I can hold Hansel's illusion until he can escape. He'll be devastated over the loss of his little sister. I'm responsible for her death now.

"Get out of here, Hansel," I will him, whispering as guards pound against the wall, some nearby. "Don't be stupid. Go get Aurik and Brahms and leave. Come back and kill the king another day."

I can't believe we had come so close only to have him be pulled out of Gretel's grasp before she had ended him. She only had him under her control for a moment before the guard interrupted her, but it wasn't quite long enough. It was much easier for her to create life than death.

"Gretel? Gretel, I need you to come back to me," I beg, but I'm not Hansel and I have no control over life and light.

I wheel us around a corner, trusting the illusion walls to take us out of the palace by way of the main entrance —it's the only way I knew to get out.

Maybe, by some miracle, I can reach the end before the guards do and transform Gretel back into a young girl, fulfilling her request to look like me. And if by some miracle, I can, maybe Hansel will be there to pull her to safety.

I have to hope.

Light starts to filter into the tunnel I've created, and I assume we're reaching the end, but the noise behind me assures me I'll never make it—the guards have broken in and are running behind us.

Tears blur my vision as Gretel stares back blankly at me. Then, she blinks.

Perhaps she's coming back.

Moving my wrist to take the pressure of pushing the cake, I wiggle my fingers at her, dropping the illusion I'd placed over her. Her skin bounces back, tightening. Brunette locks color in the gray mats as Gretel returns to me.

But two women entered the tunnel—one of them was a witch.

The men gain on me. Another few steps and they will know.

I do the only thing I can—I transform.

CHAPTER 9

I cover the tunnel in candies of every color as I work to change everything the guards will see. I bring my candy-world to life again, hoping to distract them. At the very least, I hope they trip over some of it.

A man slams into me, knocking me to the ground. Gretel careens forward, slamming into the wall that turns at a ninety-degree angle, jutting out into the courtyard. I kick the man off me, scrambling to reach Gretel. My screams fill the hollow hallways, echoing out into the courtyard.

Hansel has one chance of saving his sister, and it's now.

I drop all of the illusions but the ones that cling to my body and to Hansel and Gretel. The walls disappear, but the candy bounces on the ground around us, reappearing. Brunette-Gretel—nearly unrecognizable—sits in a pile on the ground, free from the cake debris. Somewhere, Hansel is in his illusion form, looking for a way to us. Light floods around us and I squint.

"The witch!" one of the men shouts.

"She put a girl in the cake!"

"How did she get her?" another shouts.

People pull at Gretel, trying to get her away from the evil witch rising from the ground. Hands pull at her, and I want to stop them, but I can't draw extra attention to her.

"The witch was trying to eat the child!" someone screams. "She couldn't have the king's soul, so she tried to take the little girl's!"

"Stand back!" A man's voice shouts. It's familiar. "She'll steal your souls too!"

Bauer rushes toward Gretel and pulls her from a woman's hand. The boys must have been able to release him in the chaos of the king's almost-death. I move my fingers, concealing our leader in an illusion so the guards don't recognize him. He nods once to me, reinforcing the decision I made. Someone will pay the price, and it's going to be me.

Aurik and Brahms stand off to the side, trying to

assess the scene. They haven't caught on yet, but they watch Bauer—they saw him transform, so they know I'm here somewhere—and take his lead as he clings to Gretel. They know the brunette girl isn't me, but they haven't figured out I switched places with the girl yet.

The guards draw their weapons, kicking the illusion candy out of the way.

"You can't kill a witch, you fools," Bauer shouts. The boys echo him, realizing where I am as they try to spare me an immediate death.

The crowd is fearful of me, holding their children behind their backs, trying to move as far away as possible without catching the attention of the men wielding weapons. Any movement toward or away from me could be taken as a sign of their involvement—either to help the witch or run from their crimes connected to the hag that tried to kill the king and nearly sucked the soul from a small girl.

A guard calls to me, trying to talk me into kneeling and giving up. As long as Hansel isn't here to save Gretel, I can't give up yet, no matter what that means.

Searing pain rips through my arm as one of the guards shoots at me. It tears through my flesh, and blood spills out, dousing my black lace sleeve. Better me than Gretel.

Bauer pulls Gretel deeper into the crowd. She steps back with him, but she's still not with us.

"Witch!" the deep-voiced guard calls to me, reminding me once again of my father's voice. "You are accused of trying to kill the king of Candestrachen. The punishment is death."

Oddly enough, I'm about to take Bauer's place. At least the resistance has their leader back—I'm of no use to them anymore now anyway—we've played my card.

A flash of red grabs my attention—Hansel is here.

I look him in the eye and tap my necklace. He registers my height—much taller than Gretel—and realizes that I'm taking her place. He locks eyes with me and his face falls. Hansel shakes his head once, begging me to find another way, but I can't; not from this.

"Witch!" the deep-voiced man calls again. "Give up."

I dip my hands to the sides, stretching out my arms, but I say nothing. Hansel's gaze follows my more emphasized arm to where his sister's necklace gleams in the light. His pendant glints as he rushes to her side.

Bauer says something to Hansel, letting him know he's in an illusion, preventing him from ripping his sister away unnecessarily. I see them as I slowly spin in a circle, taking in the crowd.

This is the last time I'll see the sun or breathe the fresh air. It's the last time I'll feel dirt under my feet, and the final time I'll see people. I take it all in. Closing my eyes for a moment, I inhale, filling my lungs.

When I open my eyes, I complete my circle. I stare

down the guard, daring him to come for me. I don't speak.

He takes a strong step forward, thinking I'll balk. I don't.

"You'll die for this, Witch. You'll be taken before the king. You'll pay for this."

I wave my hand and the candy littering the courtyard disappears.

I'm sure I will pay for this.

At least I'll get to see what has become of the half-dead king in person. I'll know how soon they'll all be safe from him in his weakened state.

Weapons are raised in my direction again, but the guard instructs them not to kill me yet. The king, of course, will want his say in the matter.

"He's alive, Witch. You didn't kill him, but you knew that, didn't you? That's why you stole the child."

With all eyes on me, I drop Hansel and Gretel's illusions, leaving them in their true forms. The little girl the witch tried to devour is no more—they'll never find the brunette again.

The guards run at me, tackling me. Screams rise up in the crowd as they kick me, mingling with my own. I'm wrenched backward, onto my knees to face the crowd.

"This is what happens when you come against the king!" He rips my hair back, tears pressing against my open eyes as I snarl. I must look hideous in this form when I make that face.

Hansel looks devastated, hands wrapped tightly around Gretel as if she's the only thing anchoring him to this world. He rocks on his feet, leaning forward with her. She's the only barrier keeping him from running to save me.

Aurik places a hand on Hansel's arm, ready to make the decision for him if he needs to—escape comes first. Bauer prepares to back him up if necessary.

Gretel blinks, slowly coming back as Hansel pulls her back to us. She'll register what's happening in a moment. She doesn't need to see this, and I silently will Hansel to run. I don't want her feeling responsible for me. He can tell her I was lost during the escape, but not how it came to be—he'll protect her from this, but he can't if she sees with her own eyes.

Hansel's beautiful hair falls over his face, catching the light just enough to make him glow, but then, Hansel has always been full of light. He radiates everywhere he goes and illuminates the path for every life he touches. I regret not spending more time with him earlier on.

He's breathing heavily as he watches me. A tear slips down his cheek. His lips part in a silent prayer.

I try to smile. I want him to know I'll be all right. I want to do this for them.

He shakes his head, disappointed that everything

crumbled around us like a candy house smashed by a child's errant fist. Tears stream down his face—he knows there's nothing he can do.

Bauer tugs him back—it's time for them to go.

I nod and blink back tears.

Bauer and Aurik pull Hansel back, fighting him. Brahms wraps Gretel in his arms and pulls her away just as she comes out of her trance. He shields her from the horrors around her. Hansel strains against his friends. Giving up, he finally bows his head, a complete wreck.

"I'm sorry," he mouths to me, disappearing in the crowd as they force him away. He reaches for me, hand disappearing behind the crowd.

The guards beat me, forcing my body to jerk in different ways until they lift me off my feet.

Hansel and Gretel will try again. Bauer will come up with a new plan. The bakery will likely be taken over by one of the other girls in our group of rebels that can pass as me, but I doubt Hansel and Gretel will ever set foot in it again. Life will go on without me for the rebels and for Hansel and Gretel.

My fate is uncertain. Should the king lock me in one of his prisons before my execution, I'll decorate it in illusions and slip away in my mind, oblivious to what will happen to me. If he kills me on the spot, it will all be over. The fireworks this evening will signal the destruction of the witch that kills kings and eats the souls of children.

I was never a witch, but if I must take the fall to protect Hansel and Gretel, I'll be whatever kind of monster Levin needs me to be.

I contributed to the cause, and now the king is aged so dramatically that even if the resistance fails again, Levin only has a few years at most. Our people will see his candy-colored world crumbles around him, even if I'm not here to see it through.

I wave my hands at the sky, setting off illusion fireworks that end in shattered pieces of candy bouncing off the rooftops of Candestrachen—my final goodbye to the world I'm giving my life to protect.

I can't sugarcoat their world anymore.

Acknowledgements

Sorry. I know that ending was mean.

If you've followed along with any of my other books, you probably saw it coming…I wish I could say one day I'd write fluff instead of a realistic ending, but I just don't think that's going to be a thing. Besides, who doesn't love a tragic love story, right?

I hope you all enjoyed Annika and Hansel's heartbreaking love story as much as I did. I wrote this during a pretty rough time and I needed a few extra kissing scenes in my life, so you're welcome. I hope their sugarcoated romance was just what you needed in your life too!

I've always been huge fan of twisted villain tales where we discover the hero lied and changed the story, so when we created a villains anthology, I was thrilled to get to explore the darker side of a fairytale.

Sugarcoated didn't have a name for the longest time and it kind of fell into place as I was writing—it couldn't be a more perfect name for Annika's tale. Once that clicked, everything else worked out easily. I adore Annika and Gretel, and their fierce girl power vibes, and Hansel has certainly made his way high on my list of swoony leading men I've written.

Speaking of which, if you loved him as much as I did, send me an email or direct message and let me know so we can gush over him together!

Special thanks to Elle and Jess for all of their help with Sugarcoated. Thank you to Jessica for all the fun commentary (I appreciate you not threatening to pull my hair this time!)

And to you, oh lovely reader, thank you for coming on this journey with me. I don't write fantasy often, but this candy-coated world of mine has been a joy to live in! I hope you found this book just as sweet as I did!

Be sure to hit up my website for more from the world of Sugarcoated!

Stay inspired!

-K.M. Robinson

WORLD PORTALS

Ready to learn exclusive facts about Sugarcoated and other K.M. Robinson Series?

World Portals are now available on
www.kmrobinsonbooks.com

Learn behind the scenes facts, watch videos, play games, check out our book filters, find out where to get bonus scenes, view fan art, and get access to other secrets we've hidden away inside the World Portals on the website.

You can also see the map that we weren't able to add to this version of the story due to file size limits.

The World Portals are constantly changing and information is being taken away and added all the time, so check back frequently for new content!

146

ABOUT THE AUTHOR

K.M. Robinson is a storyteller who creates new worlds both in her writing and in her fine arts conceptual photography. She is a marketing, branding and social media strategy educator who is recognized at first sight by her very long hair. She is a creative who focuses on photography, videography, couture dress making, and writing to express the stories she needs to tell. She almost always has a camera within reach. Visit her at her website: www.kmrobinsonbooks.com

CONNECT ON SOCIAL MEDIA

facebook.com/kmrobinsonbooks

instagram.com/kmrobinsonbooks

twitter.com/kmrobinsonbooks

Get free books and excerpts of other K.M. Robinson
books at excerpt.kmrobinsonbooks.com

Along Came A Spider: A Prequel Novelette

And They'll Come Home: A Prequel Novelette

The Archives of Jack Frost Series

The Revolution of Jack Frost

The Redemption of Jack Frost (coming soon)

Virtually Sleeping Beauty: A Novella Retelling

The Goose Girl and The Artificial: A Novella Retelling

The Sinking: A Novella Retelling

Cindrill (coming soon)

JADED: BOOK ONE OF THE JADED DUOLOGY

Her father failed in his mission to take control from the Commander, a defeat that has cost Jade her life. She will die as punishment. Now she belongs to the Commander's son—as his wife. Knowing his intent is to quietly kill her in revenge, Jade's every move is calculated to survive—until she learns her death ensures the safety of her father and her entire town.

Roan doesn't want to kill Jade, but once his family isolates her from her father and community, his only choice is to go through with the plan. Jade doesn't make it easy as she tries to sway him into falling for her. Each misstep makes him question his cause. Each moment makes every decision harder, but the Commander won't allow him to fail.

One chooses life. One chooses death. In the midst of the chaos, only one will succeed.

Now available!
Learn more about The Jaded Duology at
jadedinfo.kmrobinsonbooks.com

GOLDEN: BOOK ONE OF THE GOLDEN TRILOGY

Goldilocks was never naive. She was sent on a mission and Dov Baer is her new target.

When the girl with the golden hair betrays everyone, not even she has hope of surviving.

The stories say that Goldilocks was a naïve girl who wandered into a house one day. Those stories were wrong. She was never naïve. It was all a perfectly executed plan to get her into the Baers' group to destroy them.

Trained by her cousin, Lowell, and handler, Shadoe, Auluria's mission is to destroy the Baers by getting close to the youngest brother, Dov, his brother and sister-in-law and the leaders of the Baers' group.

When she realizes Dov isn't as evil as her cousin led her to believe, she must figure out how to play both sides or her deception will cause everyone in her world to burn.

If her allegiances are discovered, either side could destroy her...if the Society doesn't get her first.

Available now!

Learn more about The Golden Trilogy at

goldeninfo.kmrobinsonbooks.com

THE SIREN WARS: BOOK ONE OF THE SIREN WARS SAGA

War has hovered around the kingdom of Scylla for generations ever since the original sirens left the mer collection generations ago after nearly drowning the human prince. Over the years, select mermaids from the royal bloodline have been trained as spies to work for the reigning kings and queens, keeping the collection safe from sirens and humans.

Celena and her partner, Merrick, work covertly for the royals—not even her twin brother knows. When they discover the sirens have broken through the barriers the mer set up to keep the sirens out, Celena and her friends must race to the old kingdom of Metten to stop them from starting a war within their borders.

When she's dragged to the surface, Celena realizes that the war above the waters is as deadly as the one below the waves—and sacrificing herself may be the only way to protect her family.

The Siren Wars have only just begun.

Available now!
Learn more about The Siren Wars Saga at
sirenwarsinfo.kmrobinsonbooks.com

ALONG CAME A SPIDER: THE FIRST PREQUEL NOVELETTE TO THE LEGENDS CHRONICLES

Little Hacker Muffet

sat on her tuffet

destroying her cords and Way.

Along came a hacker named Spider,

who sat down beside her

and frightened his opponent away.

When Fet, one of the most skilled hackers in the Legends, discovers her best friend and leader of her group has been abducted and held for ransom, she must escape unnoticed and find Peep before it's too late.

When Spider, a new recruit training to join her hacker

ring, slips out with her and claims to have a plan to save her friend, Fet is forced to bring him along. As she discovers he's not who he claims to be, she faces grave danger and learns just how deadly a spider bite can be.

Now available!
Learn more about The Legends Chronicles at
acasinfo.kmrobinsonbooks.com

VIRTUALLY SLEEPING BEAUTY

She may be doing battle in the virtual world, but in the real world, they can't wake her up…

All Rora wants is to help people as class president, give her time to local charities, and quietly earn her way to the top level of the virtual reality system that the entire country uses without anyone noticing she's the second best player in the game.

All Royce wants to do is level up as a knight inside the gaming system, slay dragons, and eventually play his way to controlling the palace as he takes the crown away from the reigning queen.

When his Aunt Perry calls him, hysterically screaming that her goddaughter, Rora, has been inside for more than the four hours the game allows, Royce rushes over to help.

Entering the game, Royce soon discovers that Rora is trapped inside the system after an encounter with an evil magician who can change forms inside the game and control the virtual world. If he and his friend can't help her beat the game, she might not be able to wake up in the real world at all.

When virtual knights and princesses meet to slay dragons and defeat evil rulers, there's nothing stopping them from suffering real-world consequences too.

To wake her up, he must enter the game and help her beat it.

Now available!
Learn more about Virtually Sleeping Beauty at
vsbinfo.kmrobinsonbooks.com

THE REVOLUTION OF JACK FROST

No one inside the snow globe knows that Morozoko Industries is controlling their weather, testing them to form a stronger race that can survive the fall out from the bombs being dropped in the outside world—all they know is that they must survive the harsh Winter that lasts a month and use the few days of Spring, Summer, and Fall to gather enough supplies to survive.

When the seasons start shifting, Genesis and Jack know something is going on. As their team begins to find technology that they don't have access to inside their snow globe of a world, it begins to look more and more like one of their own is working against them.

. . .

Genesis soon discovers Morozoko Industries, but when a foreign enemy tries to destroy their weather program to make sure their destructive life-altering bombs succeed in destroying the outside world, only one person can shut down the machine that is spinning out of control and save the lives of everyone inside the bunker—Jack.

Now available!
Learn more about The Revolution of Jack Frost at
jackfrostinfo.kmrobinsonbooks.com

THE SINKING

The sea with wants to silence her, but not for the reason you think.

When a quirky older woman pawns a fancy seashell necklace at her mother's antique shop on the pier, Cara doesn't think much about the story the woman spins about the wearer turning into a mermaid.

On her way home, she accidentally drops the necklace into the ocean and is swept out to sea where she meets Quay--a merman who volunteers to take her to his mother, the sea queen, to help her get her legs back.

. . .

Cara soon learns that it's Quay's eighteen birthday--a day that has been a curse for his family--and is meant to be one for her too. Now she must fight to survive the sea with Quay at her side.

Fans of The Little Mermaid will love this twisted take on the beloved story.

Now available!
Learn more about The Sinking at
thesinkinginfo.kmrobinsonbooks.com

CINDRILL

Cinderella is an assassin out to murder the prince...but he's hunting her too.

The nanobots Cindrill's master gives her to use as a mask allow her to slip into the ball wearing a face that isn't hers, but when the assassination attempt goes sideways, Prince Davin doesn't understand why her face changes when he injures her, slicing her foot open around a unique pair of shoes as she runs away.

When Cindrill runs into the prince the next day without her nanobot mask on, he doesn't recognize her, but immediately decides her skills will be useful on his hunt for the would-be-assassin woman who nearly killed his father and his fiancée the night before.

Both are tasked with the job of murdering the other, but things don't quite go as they had planned when Cindrill's master and Davian's fiancée interfere as the two try to decide whether or not to kill the other.

It's hard to recognize a woman when she uses technology to change her appearance, but Cindrill is going to use that to her full advantage as she destroys the prince. Will either survive?

Learn more about Cindrill at

cindrillinfo.kmrobinsonbooks.com